AT WAR WITH A BROKEN HEART

DAHLIA DONOVAN

———HOT TREE PUBLISHING———

LIST OF BOOKS

THE GRASMERE TRILOGY:
Dead In The Garden
Dead In The Pond
Dead In The Shop

THE SIN BIN SERIES:
The Wanderer
The Caretaker
The Botanist
The Royal Marine
The Unexpected Santa
The Lion Tamer
Haka Ever After

STANDALONES:
After The Scrum
Forged In Flood
Found You
One Last Heist
The Misguided Confession
All Lathered Up
At War With A Broken Heart

At War with a Broken Heart © 2019 by Dahlia Donovan

All rights reserved. No part of this book may be used or reproduced in any written, electronic, recorded, or photocopied format without the express permission from the author or publisher as allowed under the terms and conditions with which it was purchased or as strictly permitted by applicable copyright law. Any unauthorized distribution, circulation or use of this text may be a direct infringement of the author's rights, and those responsible may be liable in law accordingly. Thank you for respecting the work of this author.

At War with a Broken Heart is a work of fiction. All names, characters, events and places found therein are either from the author's imagination or used fictitiously. Any similarity to persons alive or dead, actual events, locations, or organizations is entirely coincidental and not intended by the author.

For information, contact the publisher, Hot Tree Publishing.
WWW.HOTTREEPUBLISHING.COM

EDITING: HOT TREE EDITING
COVER DESIGNER: SOXSATIONAL COVER ART
FORMATTING: RMGRAPHX

ISBN: 978-1-925853-27-8

For all the Haggards in the world who offer so much to their humans.

CHAPTER ONE

FIE

"Would you stop ignoring me?"

"No."

"Morrie."

"How about you quit butchering my name? If you insist on using my first one that no one else uses, stop making me sound like a five-year-old schoolboy. It's Morogh, though you know I prefer Fie." Morogh Fie Russell scowled at the former love of his life over the top of his reading glasses. He hadn't seen Edmund in close to eight years, not since Fie's return from Afghanistan. War hadn't been kind to him, leaving him a changed man in many ways. "I'll ignore you if I want, as I didn't invite you inside."

"I refuse to call you by a name that sounds like it belongs in *Jack and the Beanstalk*. What were your parents thinking?" Edmund took a few steps towards Fie, grimacing when he stepped into a stray bit of wet clay. "I wanted to talk. How do you stand it out here in Bideford? I'm surprised you didn't move back to your family's farm in Scotland. Devon doesn't seem your sort of place."

"You refused to call me anything at all for years. And how is where I live any of your business?" Fie honestly didn't want to revisit their failed relationship. "What's changed? Did your latest fling kick you out?"

"I missed you. Us, even." Edmund gestured towards Haggard, Fie's blue merle border collie service dog, stretched out across a blanket in his corner of the pottery shed. "I can help. What can your old mutt do that I can't?"

"Help? You broke me. You lost the right to put me back together." Fie wiped absently at the sheen of sweat on his brow; he hadn't even gotten close to his kiln yet. *Why am I suddenly overheating?* "Sod off with you back to your posh London penthouse."

"I'm sorry."

"Hell." Fie dragged a hand roughly through his greying hair. His dark brown eyes examined Edmund and found him relatively unchanged. *Still as selfish as ever.* He'd missed seeing the fault in his ex-lover's personality until far too late. "Well, I hope the apology made it all better for you. I still feel like shite."

"I'm sorry." Edmund was trying for heartfelt, but it came out sulky to Fie.

"You sent me off to war with a broken heart." Fie stood up suddenly, knocking his stool over. He dwarfed

Edmund with his tall, bulky, almost bearlike frame. "Now I'm shipping you off to London. I imagine it's far less dangerous than disarming explosives in the desert, and you're certainly not as emotionally shattered as I was."

Getting up from his sleep, Haggard trotted over to plop himself down next to Fie. As if timed by the dog and his music player, strains of his Merle Haggard playlist started up. He reached down to pick up his chair and sat on it.

Staying calm had become such a difficult concept for him since his return. Fie had lots of pamphlets about post-traumatic stress; he'd never read most of them. He'd taken to the dog better than the therapy.

"I can't believe you're just going to throw away what we had." Edmund had never been the most self-aware individual. "Why won't you even try?"

"You do remember you dumped my arse? Right?"

"How can you listen to this American rubbish?" Edmund changed the subject rapidly, likely in an attempt to give himself time to think.

"It relaxes me." Fie glanced over at the clock on the wall. "Was there anything else? I've got to get started on some new mugs."

There wasn't anything else.

All their words had been said. Fie certainly remembered every painful, callous moment. He'd gone to Afghanistan with a gaping hole in his heart and returned with an even larger one.

Fie had hoped to marry Edmund one day—if it became legal. He'd been on top of the world with a solid military career and a boyfriend. Then, just days before his next flight overseas, he'd been dumped with hardly any explanation at all.

What does "I want more from life" even mean?

Insecurity had followed him to Afghanistan.

It took a while for Edmund to take the hint and leave, Fie hoped for good. He had no interest in ever seeing his former lover again.

With his morning wasted, Fie tried to get ahead on an order for coffee mugs from a bed and breakfast a few villages over. He'd always loved pottery, but after the war, creating things with his hands had brought him a tiny amount of peace. Handle with Care was the perfect name for his shop.

Good advice as well for both his mugs and for himself.

With the newest batch in the kiln, Fie decided to treat himself to a fresh cup of coffee. *I could make it, but Davet's is so much better.* He hesitated. He'd already been once today, and the queue around this time would likely be overwhelming for him.

Haggard was suddenly at his feet, paw resting on Fie's shoe.

"Want to go for a walk then? I swear you're psychic."

Haggard and his shop had come together at about the same time. Fie had wanted to do something with the money earned and had discovered in the process of getting a therapy dog how difficult it could be for returning veterans to gain access to one. Handle with Care donated a significant portion of profits toward helping make it easier and faster.

He hadn't saved the soldiers in his command.

He'd save some now though.

"All right, then. C'mon, Haggard. Let's see if Davet saved some dog biscuits for you." Fie double-checked the kiln to ensure nothing would implode in his absence. "What can it hurt?"

The twenty-minute walk in the brisk winter air gave him time to clear his head. *And stress over the people, and cars, and sounds.* But Haggard's steady presence at his side kept him grounded. Fie still occasionally dealt with flashbacks from the explosion that had taken his first dog and several of the soldiers in his command from him. As a result, he avoided driving when at all possible.

Coffee First, more drink stall than an actual café, was set up in the tiniest of houses. Fie remembered the first time it opened for business; Davet had been equal parts suave and flustered while making Fie's drink, introducing himself with the barest hint of a French accent.

Davet had run his little stall for almost two years now. He'd initially lived with his younger brother at a nearby cottage owned by their uncle, but Fraco had gone off to university. Though Fie had never pressed them for their story, he had a sneaking suspicion they'd run away from something.

A friendship had slowly developed between him and Davet over early morning coffee runs. Fie preferred not to get stuck with loads of people. They meant well, but always wanted to pet Haggard. Or worse, they'd ask about his service.

Unlike the other residents, Davet never judged Fie for his lapses in good humour. He handled his abruptness as if used to it. Then again, both Davet and his brother were proudly autistic; they had some experience with neural struggles.

Most mornings, Davet had a mug and a muffin waiting for Fie. They'd listen to the birds, have breakfast, and natter about nothing important. On especially cold days they drank inside the cottage. Sometimes, they talked about Fraco's adventures studying agriculture at university.

"Are you early or late? You've missed Detective Sid. He picked up his coffee an hour ago." Davet smiled brightly when Fie made it up to the front of the line. "I don't generally see you in the afternoon. Did you skip lunch again?"

Fie flinched when someone further back in the queue shrieked with laughter. *I should've made my own coffee.* "I...."

Davet watched him struggling to find words while controlling the urge to fight or flee. "I've had trouble all morning with this one box. It's a bit heavy. Can you give me a hand?"

Without even getting a chance to respond, Fie found himself inside the tiny house, in a room with loads of books, posters of animals, and a stack of CDs and a player. Davet gestured toward the chair crammed in the corner and handed over headphones. Haggard curled up nearby, keeping an eye on his charge.

"Sometimes my brother and I struggle. He has more trouble than I do. This helps. I know it's not the same, but it might do you good." Davet disappeared, only to return with a cup of coffee and a freshly baked muffin. "Just don't let Haggard eat the rabbit."

Unlike Fie's family, who tended to hover, Davet left him alone. He didn't throw a million questions at him. It allowed him space to breathe.

Wait.
Rabbit?
When did he get a rabbit?

CHAPTER TWO

DAVET

"Get a hold of yourself." Davet grimaced at the hot coffee dripping from the counter onto his already damp shoes. He'd spilt four cups in the last hour since Fie took refuge in his quiet room. "What in the world is wrong with me?"

He dragged a hand through his slightly wavy black hair. His hazel eyes took in the new mess he'd made with a groan. *I know I can be clumsy, but this is beyond ridiculous.*

Davet and his little brother had against all the odds inherited their dark hair and olive-toned skin from their mother's Spanish family. It had skipped a generation. He'd always been proud of their mixed heritage—his mother and father, not so much.

All right, let's work on cleaning up and stop obsessing with whether or not Fie finds me attractive.

He doesn't.

Stop it.

Despite almost two years of friendship, Davet still managed to get flustered by Fie's mere presence. He remembered vividly the first time they'd met. It had been the day after the shop's opening.

Each morning after, Fie showed up earlier and earlier. Davet had been initially puzzled. He'd eventually realised the big bear of a man wanted to avoid people.

Not Davet, but everyone else in the village who wanted coffee in the early hours of the morning. It was a sentiment he understood intimately, as an autistic, and the guardian of one. He and his younger brother, Fraco, were both on the spectrum.

Fraco tended to struggle socially more than he. He liked Fie, though. They both did.

Fie, who showed up at six in the morning with his empty mug and his dog.

Fie, who disappeared the second another customer arrived an hour later.

And my constant drooling over his deliciously bulky body and haunting brown eyes has nothing to do with it.

And there goes another cup of coffee.

Merde.

But mother of God is he— Focus, Davet, or you'll never get this cup out to the customer.

Coffee had always been an obsession of his. When Davet moved his little brother to Bideford, their uncle had offered them the land, the tiny house on it, and a series of picnic tables. And Coffee First had been born from pondering what to do with himself.

Customers brought their own mugs or used the ones he'd commissioned from Fie's pottery last year. They sat, drank their coffee, and usually gossiped with each other. Davet went out of his way to ensure his brew was the best in town.

Their first year of living in Bideford, Davet had gotten close with Shirley, who ran a nearby bakery. She frequently brought baskets of muffins and scones for him to sell along with his coffee. He always saved two glazed orange scones, one for himself and the other for Fie.

And now I'm back to thinking about him again.

As his customers dwindled, Davet decided to check in on his bear. *Guest, guest. And he's not my anything. Not yet.* He glanced at his reflection in the gleaming espresso machine, yanking off his beanie and dragging a hand roughly through his ink-black hair. He stared absently at the coffee molecule tattoo on his neck before shaking his head at his own ridiculous vanity.

Just because Fie has taken refuge in my sanctuary doesn't mean he's suddenly going to profess an uncontrollable attraction to me.

Might be nice if he did, though.

"Fie?" Davet tapped lightly before stepping into the room. He froze immediately when a strong arm pushed him against the wall. Fie's eyes seemed unfocused, and his service dog appeared to be attempting to distract him. "Hello, Haggard. Did you eat the rabbit yet? Aren't you such a good puppy?"

Fie slowly released him while Davet continued to chat with the collie at their feet. "Shite," he muttered.

Davet stayed by the door, keeping his voice soft and allowing the clearly disoriented Fie to collect himself. "Want a scone?"

"Might be best if I go home now." Fie dropped his hand to Haggard's head to ruffle his fur. "I'm sorry."

Davet waved off the apology; he didn't believe one was owed. "See you in the morning? Shirley's promised to bring the extra orange-y scones for us."

"Tomorrow?"

"Yes." Davet offered a bright smile to hopefully assure him of a warm welcome. "Tomorrow. Coffee in the morning, as always."

With Haggard following close at his heels, Fie trudged by him without another word. Davet didn't take the silence personally. He had times when even a quick "hello" seemed too much to process.

To combat that particular issue while working, Davet opened and closed earlier than most cafés. He often spent the rest of the day decompressing, or he'd hop in his old VW Polo to drive out to see his brother.

Fraco had moved into a new place with roommates to attend university, and Davet worried. His brother hadn't been away from him—ever. They were both struggling with the change.

He reminded himself frequently that his brother was no longer a child. Fraco didn't *need* him to be there to chase away the nightmares. And still, he worried.

They'd managed to fight through so much together on their own.

But I worry.
I do.
I just want this move to work—for both of us.

"Am I too late for coffee?"

Davet peered out the window to see Detective Inspector Sidney Little holding up his coffee mug with an easy smile. "How many have you already had?"

"Only two of yours." Sid moved closer, lifting up the mug between both of his hands. "I'm stuck on a terribly long shift. Please, sir, can I have some more?"

Davet flushed at the smile directed his way from his other village crush. "I'll make yours extra strong."

Steeling himself for the usual end of the workday grind, Davet spent hours cleaning up and preparing for the following morning. He had his music turned on to keep away the drudgery. Coffee was fun; everything else wasn't.

His cottage looked more like a tiny house with a commercial kitchenette attached to the front and an awning over a large window that looked out across the various tables. When the weather permitted, Davet kept the window open to take orders through it. He enjoyed the stiff breeze as well; helped him stay awake when coffee couldn't.

It was rather small, but it was home. More so than the tiny place in Paris where they'd lived previously, and certainly leaps and bounds better than being with their parents in the French countryside. He had no regrets about moving to Devon.

Taking Fraco with him had required an extended battle in court. Davet had been lucky that his godfather happened to be a lawyer who specialised in family law. He'd fought to take his brother from his parents, and after two years he'd finally won.

He only regretted how long it had taken. They'd easily proved how unfit his parents were. It had been demonstrating his ability to care for Fraco that had required relentless work on his part.

With his mother's family in Devon, Davet had hoped the distance would prove enough of a barrier to their parents. Thus far, they'd both stayed away from their sons. He hoped it continued.

In their two years in Devon, Fraco had finally started to flourish. He'd indulged his love of animals and earned himself a spot at the nearby university studying agriculture. Their uncle Santos had a place at a local farm already lined up for him to work after graduation.

Fraco loved animals more than people. "Except you, Davet," he always said. Most days, Davet believed his younger brother.

"Davet?"

He paused in wiping down one of the picnic tables to find his uncle and one of the local police officers making their way slowly toward him. He watched his uncle say something, but only the wind sounded in his ears. "Pardon?"

"Sit down, Davet."

"Non." He shook his head, pulling away from his uncle as he reached out to him. "No."

"Davet." Santos took a few steps toward him. "Davet, please. We have to tell you—"

"You don't."

"I'm so sorry, son. So sorry." His uncle caught him by the shoulders to hold him in place. "They found Fraco in the canal."

"He can't swim."

"Fraco had an… accident." His uncle struggled to finish his sentence. "He didn't make it."

"He's in the hospital?" Davet heard the rush of wind starting to return; he swayed on his feet while completely forgetting how to breathe. "He'll be fine."

"No, I'm afraid he won't be fine. They found him too late." Santos wrapped him tightly in a hug but released him when Davet struggled against the embrace. "I'm so sorry. I'm so bloody sorry."

Davet's legs went out from under him and he dropped to his knees in the damp grass. "He can't swim. He hates water. It's the middle of winter. Why was he out there?"

"I don't know."

"Tell me why," Davet screamed at his uncle. "Why?"

CHAPTER THREE

Fie

Sleep evaded him. Fie tossed and turned all night in remembered embarrassment over the incident at the coffee shop. He eventually gave up at four in the morning to drag himself into his workshop to channel his emotional turmoil into a mug or two.

It helped, mostly.

Why the bloody hell have I let Edmund throw me for a loop once again?

The trouble with Edmund was that along with him came a flood of memories from the months after their break-up. And Fie had done his best to put those days behind him. He'd never forget, couldn't, but he didn't want to drown in regret either.

As usual, the siren call of coffee dragged him away from darker thoughts. Fie grabbed his usual mug, whistled for Haggard, and headed out the door. Davet usually had a pot on for him even before the shop opened, a kind gesture from the young entrepreneur who always appeared to enjoy his company in the early morning hours.

And I should definitely not read anything into that.

And what was there to read anyway?

Why would he be interested in a broken-down soldier like me?

In all honesty, Fie hadn't dated since the break-up with Edmund what felt like a century ago. At first, he'd hesitated to even consider a romantic entanglement until his emotions, stress, and depression had been sorted out. But then, as each year dragged by, he'd settled into a languid state of not having to bother.

And he hadn't missed dating, not until recently.

Wrapped up in his thoughts, Fie found himself at the gate before the path leading up to Coffee First. Haggard easily leapt over it, taking off at top speed then looping around to check on him. His fur-covered best mate always took his job as a therapy nurse seriously.

"Where is he?" Fie found all the tables empty and the cottage itself dark. "Davet?"

He walked over to the front door and knocked lightly on it. He didn't want to wake Davet up, but they'd had the same routine for ages. Something about the situation seemed off.

Haggard darted around, then bumped up into him in his usual move to get his attention.

"You're not Lassie." Fie chuckled when his dog stared back at him. "Fine, you're closely related, and

I'll follow you."

They'd barely rounded the corner of the little house when the sound of crying reached his ears. The broken sobs spoke to him of utter devastation. *Ah, hell.* Fie had personal experience with that level of loss.

Damn it.

Let's hope I don't cock this comfort thing up.

Davet sat on the grass, leaning against a portion of the brick wall that closed in the garden. He had his legs pulled up and his face buried in a blanket. A line of shattered mugs littered either side of him, a visceral demonstration of whatever loss he'd suffered.

"Can we sit with you?" Fie hesitated, not wanting to intrude but also wanting to avoid the broken pottery. "Or, better yet, let's get you inside, all right? We can clean all this up later. Have you been out here long?"

Davet didn't acknowledge his presence initially. He finally glanced up with red-rimmed eyes and coughed a few times, sounding hoarse. "He's dead."

Fie waited patiently.

"Dead." Davet slammed his fist on the ground, narrowly missing a jagged red shard. "Dead. In the canal. Dead. We fought so hard to get here for a better life—to live free. And he's gone. Just gone. He hated water. Couldn't swim. Why? Just why the fucking hell was he even near it?"

Fuck.

Breathing through the emotions threatening to overwhelm him, Fie tried to remember that Davet mattered most. Fraco had been such a sweet lad. He'd liked the young man a great deal.

Fie crouched down when the shouting switched to breathlessly weeping into the blanket. It was a duvet he'd often seen Davet's younger brother holding. "I won't say sorry. It never meant a damn thing to me when people threw their condolences at me. It bloody sucks, and I've broad enough shoulders to take all the screaming you've left to do."

"Can't." Davet pulled the duvet away from his face. He coughed repeatedly, scrubbing at the tears even though they continued to fall. "Who'd you lose?"

Fie sat back on his heels for a slightly more comfortable position. "Soldiers who were family to me. And my dog. He kept me alive, and I couldn't return the favour."

When the George's Cross had been graciously awarded to him for bravery, Fie had left the medal at the memorial of his dog, his bomb-sniffing partner. Click had deserved the acclaim. Fie had lost too many in his command to consider himself any sort of hero.

"My brother." Davet clutched the blanket to his chest, then uttered a scream that seemed ripped from his soul.

Fie winced at the raw pain and rage, but quickly caught Davet's hand when he went to slam it into the ground. "Let's get you up out of the mugs before they take their ounce of blood."

Do I pick him up?

Do I wait for him to do something?

Drops of rain made the decision for him; Fie lifted Davet off the ground away from the broken pottery. He put him on his feet, then led him into the cottage. Warmth almost immediately engulfed them, a stark difference from the frigid January air outside.

Pushing Davet onto the chair closest to the heater, Fie left Haggard to watch over him. They both needed something hot to drink. *Time for some coffee.* If nothing else, he'd be more alert to handle things.

Fie found photos scattered from the hall all the way into the kitchen. All of Fraco and Davet. He picked up a recent image from before Fraco had moved into his new flat. Davet had clearly wanted to connect with his brother through their memories.

Or worse, Davet feared forgetting his brother. He'd once explained to Fie about suffering from face blindness, an aspect of being autistic that frustrated him greatly, where Davet often struggled to recall someone, even a close loved one. It was a terrifying thought; Fie couldn't imagine dealing with the fear of never being able to recall his lost friends' faces.

I can help.

Maybe we grieve differently, but I can help.

I've a mission, and it's always best when I'm focused.

He struggled to process how Fraco had died. The young autistic had always struck him as overly cautious. His skulking around the canal made no sense at all.

Fie's cynical side was immediately suspicious of something so out of character. Both Davet and Fraco tended to be creatures of habit. He'd seen first-hand how an unexpected change of plans threw them off-kilter.

So, why now?

Putting the kettle on, Fie busied himself gathering up the photos. He set them on the counter out of the way, then hunted for the coffee which he could actually make himself. Davet's fancy machinery was a bit beyond his skills.

He'd assumed given his skills with electronics and defusing bombs that a fancy coffee machine would be a breeze. He'd been wrong. *I only broke it once.*

And he'd paid for a new one, then promised to never touch it again. Davet had kept instant coffee in one of the cupboards for him ever since.

Quit stalling.

Make the coffee.

We're going to need all the warmth and comfort we can get.

CHAPTER FOUR

Davet

The warmth from the heater did nothing to penetrate the icy fog gripping him. Davet had barely even noticed the change in temperature from coming inside. A cold numbness had sunk claws into him from the moment he'd heard the news.

He'd spent the entire night attempting to wrap his mind around Fraco never popping in to see him. No more texts at two in the morning arguing over why a particular animal wouldn't make a good pet. His constant worry over his brother being taken advantage of or bullied at university had vanished in an instant, replaced by a gaping hole of pain.

With a single whine, Haggard rested his chin on Davet's knee. The dog hadn't left his side. He huffed impatiently until Davet petted him.

"Fraco's not here." Davet held out the blanket in his hands. "What am I going to do?"

Dealing with life and people had come easier to Davet, but Fraco had always handled his emotions better. Davet fluctuated between over and underreacting. Was it normal to feel such absolute devastation when a loved one died?

Fraco.

Fraco had been his motivation to succeed with the business. Davet had done everything possible to ensure a better and safer life for them. And he had no idea how to process the burden now crushing his body so heavily that lifting a hand to pet Haggard seemed beyond him.

"Coffee?"

Davet didn't manage to raise his head when a hand appeared in front of him. "My favourite mug."

"I figured as you use this one every single morning, why break with tradition?" Fie perched awkwardly on the chair across from him and held the mug out toward Davet. "Not as good as yours, but a decent enough brew to warm us up."

Davet took the mug only to stare blankly into the coffee. He suddenly found himself struck by the image of Fraco face down in the muddy water, and his vision began to narrow. Fie reached out to grab the mug when Davet's fingers went slack. "I want to see the canal."

Fie balanced one mug on his knee and set the other on a nearby table. "Why don't Haggard and I keep you company? If you like, I can drive us."

"Fine." Davet tried to stand on shaky legs. He had no idea how to carry on without Fraco when getting to his feet seemed beyond his abilities. "I can't. I can't. How…."

Fie placed a scarred, meaty hand on Davet's knee. "One second at a time. One step after the other. Ignore the trite wankers who feed off pretending to soothe your pain with their advice. The pain of loss stays, but every inch forward, you'll find beautiful memories ease some of the agony. Fraco will always live on in those remembered moments."

"It hurts." Davet smacked his fist against his chest. "Here. Like I can't breathe deeply. Will I ever breathe again? Is this how a broken heart feels?"

Fie's fingers tightened on his knee. "Yes."

"Does it get easier to breathe?" Davet asked desperately. "Ever?"

"I don't know." He released Davet's knee and leaned back in the chair. "Some days I'm breathing easily in the sun, and other times I'm struggling for air."

Davet appreciated the blunt honesty; Fie never beat around the bush. "One breath after another."

"Until you can carry the weight of his absence without collapsing." Fie held his hand out. "Why don't I drive you?"

"Can you squeeze into my old Polo?" Davet cringed back instantly when he realised how his question sounded. "You're not too big. You're rather perfectly broad, actually. Broad- shouldered. *Broad-shouldered*. Oh my God. I'm never speaking again. Ever."

The rush of embarrassment broke through his

overwhelming grief for a moment. Fie's laughter was a ray of sun on an otherwise stormy day. Davet soaked in the warmth of it.

"I'm sure you will," Fie chuckled. He still had his hand out to Davet. "I'll squeeze just fine into your old hatchback. Why don't you have a quick shower while I sort out the broken mugs outside? You might put a note on the front door to keep anyone from annoying you."

"Customers."

Fie shrugged in response.

After focusing on inhaling and exhaling for almost a full minute, Davet latched on to Fie's hand and dragged himself to his feet. Fraco was dead. And somehow he had to discover the strength to keep going.

Shower.

I'll manage; somehow, I'll manage.

Despite the trembling in his legs, Davet managed to walk the short distance to his bedroom. He climbed into the tub fully clothed, switched on the water, and dropped to his knees with a painful thud, sobbing.

I can't do this.

I can't do this.

I can't.

Not without my brother.

Cold water pummelled his back. Davet cried until his head throbbed and his throat ached as though he'd eaten all the shards of broken mugs. He didn't know how to pick himself up even when Haggard scratched at the door.

"Davet?" Fie tapped on the door to the bathroom. "It's been thirty minutes. Haggard's going bonkers out here, which tells me you're not all right."

"Yeah," he croaked out.

"Mind if I come in?"

"Don't care." Davet's body had frozen in an awkward kneeling position in the bath. Getting out felt almost impossible.

"Right." Fie was silent for a second. "I'm opening the door."

Davet only grunted in response. What did it matter? He shivered under the continued onslaught of icy water. "Not naked."

Fie opened the door, stepped into the cramped bathroom, and spotted him. "Shite."

CHAPTER FIVE

FIE

Fie had hesitated to step into the bathroom, wanting to respect Davet's privacy. The uneasiness in the pit of his stomach along with Haggard's insistence forced him to enter. "Shite."

He's got to be freezing his arse off. Hell, he's practically turned blue.

"Let's get you warm." Fie reached over Davet to twist the knobs to get warm water flowing. His own grieving had been done mostly alone at first; maybe he could save Davet from the added struggle. "Can you shift around so you're sitting instead of kneeling?"

With the water hot and Davet seated, Fie hunted around for towels. He grabbed a couple along with a fluffy bathrobe dangling from a hook on the wall near the door. *I've imagined seeing him starkers, but this is definitely not the experience I had in mind.*

Right.

Maybe not the most useful of thoughts when he's grieving and half-frozen in the tub?

Grief.

Grief is a mindfuck.

In his heart, Fie hoped Davet never delved as deeply and darkly in his grief as Fie had. He intended to be there every step of the way. Davet and Fraco had wormed their way into his hermit life, and Fie found himself shaken by the sudden loss.

"You're not feeling better, I know, but are you warmer?" Fie crouched by the side of the tub; Davet hadn't moved an inch, even to tilt his head out of the flow of water. "Can I help you up?"

Davet didn't acknowledge him at all.

"Hell." Fie had learnt from watching the brothers that autistics tended to be incredibly protective of their personal space. He didn't want to make Davet any more stressed while trying to help. "You're going to wind up as wrinkly as an old prune."

Davet leant out of the water and peered over at Fie. "Moving is beyond my ability."

"I'm sure I can manage." Fie kept his tone light. Davet didn't need to be reminded of his loss—he'd never forget. Fie certainly hadn't. "Can I lift you?"

Davet stared at him.

"Well?"

He held a damp hand out to Fie. "Give me a lift up. If I don't move, I'll never pick myself up from this. And I can't. I just *can't.*"

"Everyone finds grief impossible to bear." Fie knew the pain of surviving when the others hadn't; it had almost killed him. "I won't tell a soul."

"My legs went numb," Davet grumbled when Fie yanked him up on his feet. He reached out to turn off the tap. "He's really gone."

Fie kept his hands on Davet when he swayed. "He is."

He shook his head, sending water flying. "I'll get changed; maybe I'll feel better in dry clothes."

Once Davet had gotten safely out of the bath, Fie left him to dry off. He wandered aimlessly around the tiny cottage. If he'd been in his own home, it would've been the perfect time for a bit of tobacco in his favourite pipe.

But not in someone else's house.

By the time Davet dried himself and changed, Fie had answered several knocks on the door from villagers wanting their morning coffee. *Why the hell can't they read the sign? It says Closed. The window is shut. Not much bloody interpretation available to it.*

And this would be why my shop never opens to the public.

His father joked about how Fie had belatedly lost the jovial nature of the Russells. He wasn't as taciturn as his maternal grandparents tended to be, but before his last deployment he'd been more like his father's side of the family.

I laughed more. I enjoyed people. Flirted with every

attractive man I met.

Haggard helped with his flashbacks and brought him out of night terrors, but his dog couldn't exactly bring his personality back. To Fie, it occasionally seemed as though his pre-Afghanistan self were a completely different human being.

It had been suffocated out of him by nightmarish memories.

He'd recovered, if only a little. Scars healed. They remained visible, at least to him, even if no one else saw them.

"I'm ready." Davet walked into the room, pulling on an oversized dark blue hoodie over his long-sleeved T-shirt. "I texted Sid."

"Sid?"

"Detective Inspector Little. He gets a double espresso with cream every morning. And one in the afternoon as well." Davet pointed to one of the larger blue mugs on the shelf. "Always in that cup. Looks like Loki, no horns or green or evilness. He's coming over to drive us because I don't know where along the canal...."

Oh, that Sid.

Brilliant.

Fie knew Sidney Little.

Intimately.

I'll have to ask him about his secret identity as an actor—or a superhero.

Maybe not with Davet grieving, though.

Fie's heart broke for Davet, who struggled to complete his sentence. "Well, you won't have to worry about my broad shoulders."

Davet blushed before grinning. His smile slowly twisted into a grimace. "Is it wrong to smile?"

"No, but you might struggle with guilt over smiling for a while. I did." Fie grabbed the coat by the door to toss over to Davet. "No freezing your arse off now I've got you warmed up."

Even now, Fie had days where survivor's guilt had him by the balls and refused to let go. He struggled with his ability to breathe when others hadn't been so lucky. With immense effort, he channelled those emotions into living the best life possible—for his friends who'd never get the chance.

"Want another coffee? Sid should be here shortly." Davet grabbed three of his to-go cups. "I'll make one for him as well."

They managed to get the coffee ready just in time for their ride to show up. Sid texted to signal his arrival. Davet had issues with car horns, mostly to do with them being loud, obnoxious, and pointless unless one happened to be driving.

"Sid." Fie spotted his blue-eyed, gingery-blond-haired friend the second he stepped outside.

"Swayze." Detective Inspector Sidney Little was definitely what Fie would call a plant. They'd served together in the military, and then randomly he'd transferred to Bideford. And they'd had one drunken night they refused to talk about. *Randomly, my arse. It's not paranoia if your friends really are conspiring against you.* "How's he managing?"

He had been a year into living in Bideford when Sid had suddenly shown up. He'd left the military a few years before Fie, choosing to work as a police detective. They generally avoided talking about why Sid had transferred to Devon from York, amongst other topics.

"He is autistic, not hearing impaired." Davet stepped out behind Fie, twisting around to lock the door. "Why are you calling him Swayze?"

"Pottery. *Ghost*. Ring a bell?" Sid was as always unmoved by the warning glare Fie sent in his direction. Davet stared at both of them in obvious confusion. "Classic movie scene from the nineties with Patrick Swayze and Demi Moore? How old are you? I'm suddenly feeling as though I've aged a hundred years."

"Old enough to use Google." Davet wandered in the general direction of Sid's vehicle with his eyes glued to his phone. "Fie doesn't look anything like Patrick Swayze. Is this a British thing?"

"You're British."

"Only half, and not even technically that. I'm more French and Spanish by way of Britain." Davet waved impatiently before holding out his phone with an image of Patrick Swayze. "I don't see any resemblance at all. Fie's hot."

Wait?

What?

I'm hot?

"Search for the pottery scene from the film." Sid sent a teasing grin at Fie, who knew his friend would be having words with him later when they were alone. "Are we ready then?"

"I still don't get it." Davet crossed his arms.

Swayze had been a nickname coined when one of their squad mates had come across a photo of Fie indulging in one of his favourite hobbies—pottery. A name that had stuck with him. He didn't mind; he knew a few soldiers with worse ones.

Much, much worse.

Tinkles and Corgi, for example.

Or Sid.

"You coming with, Swayze? Or are you planning to stand in the wind and freeze into a Swayze-sicle?" Sid stood by the front of his vehicle while Davet had already slipped into the back seat. "Will you quit glaring at me? I'm an officer of the law who isn't easily intimidated."

"Okay, MacFluff."

"You bastard."

"One good nickname reveal deserves another." Fie refused to be outdone by Sid, who'd earned his moniker from the fluffy stuffed animals his mum sent in every care package. They'd saved them up to give away to children they met. "Lead the way, MacFluff."

"Arsehole."

They kept the conversation light on the drive. Davet gazed blankly out a window, not interested in anything but his own thoughts. And who could blame him?

Life had changed forever. And now, Fie knew, Davet had to pick up the pieces of his new existence to make them work. Something far easier said than done.

CHAPTER SIX

DAVET

The drive through Bideford usually made Davet smile. He'd fallen in love with the village almost instantly. Now he saw nothing out the window, just a blur of passing colours.

When Sid veered off the road to pull up alongside the River Torridge, Davet thought his heart might shrivel up in his chest. A few stray bits of caution tape lay along the ground from where the police had blocked off the area. *Why did this seem so important earlier? I've vastly overestimated my ability to cope.*

Vastly.

Talking was impossible.

Sid twisted around in the front seat. "Take your time."

Davet inhaled deeply and reached for the door handle. He had to think through each movement to get his body to function. "Right."

Getting himself out of the vehicle, Davet found himself standing not far from one of the bridges that spanned the river. It was part of the Rolle Canal, somewhere he'd cycled to with Fraco a number of times on the Tarka Trail.

He'd appreciated the old aqueduct before, but now it loomed ominously in the distance. The beauty of the river had been tainted for him. He'd never forget what happened here.

Davet bent down to grab a stray ribbon of caution tape. He twisted it in his hands while making his way toward the edge of the river. "Was it here?"

Sid walked up beside him, stretching a hand out to gesture toward an area where the grass had been flattened and muddy footprints made a chaotic mosaic. "When I arrived, they'd brought him out of the river. He…."

Davet glanced over when Sid trailed off, seeming uncharacteristically unsure of himself. "Go on."

Sid exchanged a look with Fie, which only served to annoy Davet who struggled to figure out what their expressions were saying. "You don't want the details in your head. Remember your brother—"

"Stop it." Davet cut him off impatiently, waving his hands abruptly. "Don't coddle me. I'm not a fragile child. Tell me how you found him."

Sid glanced over at Fie for a second time.

"And quit with the knowing looks at one another. It's as rude as whispering about me so I can't hear you."

Davet scowled at the two men. He'd spent a lot of time trying to teach himself to read the expressions on non-autistics' faces but always failed miserably. "Just tell me."

Sid's eyes scanned Davet's face for a few seconds before he evidently made up his mind. "A cyclist spotted him floating in the river. His coat had gotten tangled underneath the aqueduct. He phoned 999 immediately and attempted to save Fraco's life."

"He died alone." Davet didn't need to hear the words to know Fraco hadn't come out of the water alive. "He drowned."

"We won't know for certain until the coroner sends their report." Sid followed when Davet inched down the slight incline toward a spot of trampled grass. "I'll keep you updated as much as I can."

"Blunt truth, not respectful lies to comfort me." Davet wanted to know what happened to his brother. He knew Sid might be tempted to offer a sanitised version of events. Honesty might hurt, but there'd be no lingering questions. "I don't understand why Fraco came here. At night. Into the river."

"And those are questions I intend to answer through my investigation." Sid placed a hand on Davet's shoulder. "I promise to be thorough and not stop until we know exactly what happened to your brother. Now, why don't Fie and I give you a moment alone? We'll wait for you up by the road to continue on to your brother's flat whenever you're ready."

Kneeling by the edge of the river, Davet placed his hands on the damp ground. From the muddy prints and flattened grass, he thought his brother's body had been laid there. He'd yet to fully shake the numb detachment that had settled in him.

"*Mon petit frère.*" Davet had spoken frequently in French to his brother, despite their mother insisting they use English or Spanish—her languages—as opposed to their father's. He reached into his pocket for his phone to pull up the prayer he'd searched for earlier. "Eternal rest grant unto him, O Lord, and let perpetual light shine upon him. May he rest in peace."

Religion had been one of the few areas where Davet differed from Fraco. He found any form of organised worship hard to stomach while Fraco had found a calmness through his Catholic faith. In his brother's honour, Davet thought a prayer was definitely appropriate.

If God's really up there, I hope they appreciate how fucking brilliant you are, Fraco.

If you are up there, give him rest and all the little animals to make him happy.

You owe him at least that, don't you think?

Davet brushed his jeans off a bit and took one more glance around the area. "I'll be back, Fraco. To visit with you here. I promise."

Time and weather permitting, Davet could cycle down the path to read by the river. He'd always enjoyed sitting out in the fields with Fraco. His brother would forage for animals to rescue or study with his ever-present sketch journal while Davet read his latest novel.

The thought of Fraco and his constant rescuing brought an important question to Davet's mind. What had happened to Rabbit? He knew his brother's flatmates had barely tolerated his continually bringing home injured animals to care for.

It had been the reason Fraco had brought Fox to live with him. His flatmates had refused to listen to how Rabbit and Fox had been raised together and insisted on only a single pet at a time. Davet had reluctantly agreed to take one of them.

Fox the bunny.

Davet climbed the slippery incline up to where Fie and Sid were in the middle of a hushed conversation. "We need to check on Fraco's Rabbit."

"I thought the rabbit was at your place?" Fie asked. "I saw him this morning."

"No, that's Fox."

"It's a rabbit—fluffy ears and all." Fie stared at him with what Davet assumed was confusion. "All fidgety nose, and hoppy."

"Yes, it's a rabbit named Fox." Davet hadn't been able to convince Fraco the names of his pets might confuse people.

"And the rabbit we have to check on?"

"Is a fox named Rabbit." He laughed when both men simply gawked at him. "Fraco had a unique sense of humour."

"A fox named Rabbit. And a rabbit called Fox. And they're friends?" Sid wandered around to the boot of his car and grabbed a towel that he tossed over to Davet. "This'll help with the mud on your hands and jeans."

Davet let the towel drop to the ground. "It's scratchy. Not touching it."

"How do you dry off after a shower?" Sid retrieved the towel, shaking it out before returning it to the boot. "Air?"

"Soft blanket. Or an old towel." Davet crossed his arms then glared at the detective's forehead. He usually found it easier to look above or below someone's eyes rather than into them. "Are we ready?"

"Sure." Sid scratched his head for a second. "Well, why don't we go retrieve the bunny-fox?"

"Rabbit."

"Yes, the rabbit-fox." Sid held his hand up, stopping Davet from correcting him. "Are you ready to go?"

Davet narrowed his eyes at the detective, unsure if he was being mocked or not. "Rabbit."

"If you two are done discussing whether it's a fox rabbit or a rabbit fox, are we ready to go?" Fie asked.

I'm not even close to ready.

Davet stared helplessly over his shoulder at the river. *I thought I could do this.*

Fie shifted over to stand beside him. "You're not abandoning Fraco if you leave."

"I'm not?"

CHAPTER SEVEN

Fie

"Did you know foxes did that?" Fie gaped at Rabbit—the not-bunny—as it cavorted happily around Davet. He and Sid had stayed back to allow Davet to gather his brother's belongings in peace. "The animal is more puppy than Haggard."

"Haggard's a little old man in a dog's body." Sid nodded subtly towards the three flatmates who hovered together in the corner farthest away from Davet. They were remarkably subdued. "I'm going to keep an eye on them. They barely said a word when we picked up Fraco's laptop and a few other items for our investigation."

"Here." Davet dropped the squirming fox in Fie's arms. "He's potty trained. Just don't let him run off."

"What…." Fie blinked down at the fox and up at a chuckling Sid. Haggard sat beside him, not even remotely interested in the creature. "Not one word, MacFluff."

"Who, me?" Sid leaned casually against the back of a grungy couch that would've been more at home in a tip. "Glare a bit more. It's intimidating the teenagers."

He shifted his gaze over toward the barely twenty-year-olds, who immediately averted their eyes and began whispering to each other. "Not sure they're teenagers."

"If it quacks like a duck."

"It's a duck—not a twenty-year-old punk." Fie continued to level a steady glare at the three flatmates. "Did you not see them when you did your investigation yesterday?"

"Not all of them." Sid pulled a slim notebook out of his jacket pocket. "Why don't you see how Davet is managing? I'll chat with these three and see about getting some boxes sent over."

In the process of dealing with the rabbit-fox, Davet had been informed by the three flatmates that anything left behind would be tossed out. Fie had found it difficult not to snap them like twigs. He'd restrained himself because Davet was already at the end of his rope.

Fie made his way through the flat to what had been Fraco's room, knocked on the door, then stepped inside. He waited to see if Davet would acknowledge him. Haggard stretched out on the carpet beside him.

"You don't have to do this." Davet sat on his brother's bed with piles of clothes, books, and other stuff scattered in haphazard piles around him. "I make your coffee; you don't owe me anything."

"You make me coffee before your shop is open because you know I'm more comfortable not dealing with a queue. We've chatted over breakfast for almost two years." Fie decided not to mention how on his roughest days, visiting Coffee First got him out of bed when nothing else could. "Friends help. And you're my friend."

"Friends." Davet nodded jerkily.

"Sid's called in a favour to get some boxes." Fie buried his anger at Fraco's flatmates' threats to toss his stuff. Rage wouldn't help Davet. "MacFluff's quite fond of your brother. Did you know Fraco wrote reports on animals killed on the road and filed them with the police?"

"Did he?"

"Sid took all of them." Fie had spent numerous evenings listening to his old buddy read off the reports. "Never as a joke either. He wanted Fraco to know someone cared enough to take him seriously."

"Fraco thought every living creature deserved a chance at life." Davet held a wooden rosary loosely in one hand. "I could never reconcile his faith for myself. We had similar experiences, and it made him believe more deeply. What sort of god lets a bright spirit who loves… loved everyone die in a dirty canal? Spiders. Foxes. People. Everyone."

"You're praying up the wrong crucifix." Fie had eschewed all of his mother's attempts to drag him to church. He'd seen far too much during war. "If it worked for your brother, does anything else matter?"

"I don't know." Davet dropped the rosary into a carved wooden box. "Are we friends?"

"Definitely." Fie ruthlessly silenced the part of him that wanted to scream about wanting more than friendship. There was bad timing, and then there was crassly propositioning a grieving man. "Friends."

Getting to his feet, Davet slowly peered around the cramped room. He stepped over a pile of clothing left behind by the detectives during their brief investigation. Fie watched him kneel down to start sorting them into piles.

"Folding or throwing into a box as is?" Fie asked. He crouched down near a pile of clothes. Davet hugged a bright blue shirt to his chest as tears started to flow. "Never mind me. Take your time."

Davet buried his face in the fabric and simply shook his head. "I can't do this. Fraco would be panicked to know anyone was going through his stuff. He kept everything so neat."

Fie lifted a pair of jeans from the stack beside him. "Why don't I fold all this? I have military precision down to a science."

While Davet attempted to gather himself, Fie focused on making quick work of the clothes. He methodically folded jeans, shirts, sweaters, boxers, and socks into neat, compact stacks. They all fit easily into a duffel bag he found squashed underneath Fraco's desk.

It's a start.

Davet seemed genuinely stunned by the open floor space around him. "Do they teach magic tricks in the military?"

"Not quite." Fie set the bag by the door, budging Haggard over. The dog huffed at him. "Don't you grump at me," he told him. "I'm doing the work, and you're lazing around as always."

"Do you think heaven exists?"

Fie paused while trying to organise stacks of books, all on agriculture and the care of animals, and attempted to process the question. *Do I answer honestly with a no? Or try to make him feel better? How would I have wanted the question answered?* He decided to go with honesty. "Personally? I've never believed in the pearly gates concept of the afterlife. I think we find peace. At least, I fucking hope we do."

"Peace to Fraco would've been loads of animals." Davet grabbed a photo album from the slightly crooked shelf. He flipped through it, showing Fie how most of them featured some stray creature out in the countryside around Bideford. "He never hurt a soul. Why him?"

Fie knew the unspoken question that followed. *Why not me?* He'd asked it himself for months and months after his return from Afghanistan. "There's no good answer, Davet. You'll never make sense of the whys and what-ifs. I've found you discover ways to find a sense of peace."

"Are you at peace?"

"Some days."

Usually the same time every day, at six in the morning when I'm having coffee with you. But I'll keep that to myself.

And now the silence is awkward.

Shite.

"You two in here? We've got two boxes." Sid banged into the room with the boxes. "Jacinda raided her mum's shop for a load of large travel bags. We just have to be careful with them. They'll do. She's bringing them round to give us an extra set of hands."

Between the four of them—once Jacinda arrived—they quickly gathered up all of Fraco's belongings. The three flatmates had made themselves scarce in the face of yet another detective. They waited outside until the packing was finished; Fie found their behaviour odd and Sid apparently agreed with him, based on the call he'd made to the police station to bring them in for additional questions.

"MacFluff." Fie discreetly leaned towards Sid. "Why don't we get Davet outside for some fresh air? Haggard's been glued to his side, which he usually only does to me when I'm getting too stressed."

"Ever the hero," Sid teased.

I'm no one's hero.

They emptied Fraco's room, filled up the boots of both Sid's and Jacinda's vehicles, then drove to Bideford. Davet sat silently with the rabbit-fox in his lap, and Haggard stretched out beside him. He seemed to have used up all of his words for the day.

"Santos has guests." Sid pulled up behind a shiny Porsche outside of Santos's cottage. Davet's was just behind it down a small lane, but they'd planned to leave some of the boxes with his uncle for the moment. "Definitely not a car I've seen on my rounds."

Fie watched the still silent Davet with concern while he mechanically dragged himself out of the vehicle. "C'mon, Haggard. Stop staring at the rabbit-fox like he's your new best friend."

"Davy?"

Fie frowned at the tinny voice, which set his teeth immediately on edge. He saw Davet freeze in place. Haggard growled low at the overly perfumed woman who sashayed towards him from the cottage, eyeing up both Fie and Sid. "Friends of yours?"

Davet remained silent.

"Say hello to your mother, Davy." She reached out, only to sneer when he dodged out of the way. "Don't be odd. And introduce me to your handsome friends. Have you been behaving normally for them?"

"Behaving normally?" Fie wanted to growl at the woman as Haggard continued to do.

Davet eased away from her with Fraco's playful fox in his arms. "Why are you here? Uncle Santos would've told me if you'd planned this visit."

"We're here for Fraco."

Davet shoved the fox blindly at Fie and stepped

closer to his mother. "No. You're not. You're not welcome."

"Davy."

"It's *Davet*," he snarled at her, much to Fie's surprise as he'd never seen him lose his temper.

"French."

"You named me." Davet retrieved the fox. "And I don't have to talk to you."

She went to follow Davet, but Sid and Fie stepped into her path. She batted her eyelashes at them. "It's lovely to—"

"It's really not. And you're barking up the wrong tree." Sid didn't beat around the bush. "For both of us."

"Leave Davet alone." Fie didn't see the point in even acknowledging her blatant attempt at flirtation. "He's got friends who have his back."

CHAPTER EIGHT

DAVET

All Davet wanted to do was retreat to his tiny cottage in peace with Fox and Rabbit to grieve in private for Fraco. His parents' arrival had definitely been an unwelcome fly in the ointment. He wondered what ulterior motive they had.

And they definitely had one.

They *always* had an ulterior motive.

His mother and father had never been able to hide their true nature from their sons—especially him. They always had an agenda. He knew the few years they'd been apart hadn't changed either of them.

"Why don't you leave Davet alone?" His uncle rushed out of the house, over to Davet, and gave him a kiss on the forehead. "Sorry. They showed up an hour ago. No call or anything. I tried to text you a warning."

"And Papa?" Davet hadn't seen any signs of the bully who'd made his childhood miserable.

"Inside. Bemoaning my house, the weather, and England in general." Uncle Santos glanced over his shoulder. "She hates France. He loathes all things British. Do you think they stay together out of a mutual hatred for everything?"

"Including themselves." Davet had never understood the toxic nature of his parents' relationship—with each other and their sons.

"Why don't you go with your men to the cottage?"

"Not mine."

"And you just blushed." His uncle grinned broadly at him. "Do I need to have a chat with the lads?"

"Lads?" Davet kept his voice low to avoid further embarrassment from Fie or Sid overhearing. "They're both in their thirties—maybe forties."

"Not an answer to my question."

"I'm never looking them in the eyes again if you even hint at talking to them." Davet tried to will away the flush on his neck. He glanced around his uncle at the sound of footsteps, groaning internally when he spotted his father.

"I doubt you look them in the eyes now. Them or anyone else." His father's gravelly, sneering voice made Davet shrink into himself instinctually. "Unnatural boy."

Davet forced his shoulders straight and lifted his chin up. "I am *not* a boy or unnatural for any of the reasons you always enjoy throwing at me."

"Go on, son." His uncle caught his father by the

shoulder and shoved him toward the cottage. "Head home to get the stuff sorted. Use the shed if you need more space. I'll deal with these two. Or I'll try to get them to head back to France or to a hotel or anywhere that isn't here."

"Bonne chance." Davet forced a smile.

"Buena suerte."

Leaving his uncle shouldering the load of his parental issues, Davet asked Sid to drive through the gate and down the lane towards his little cottage. He chose to walk in the hopes a brief amount of alone time would help his blush fade. It worked until he spotted Sid and Fie waiting for him.

Rabbit squirmed out of Fie's arms and raced over to Davet. *Ah, a welcome distraction.* He lifted up the fox and allowed him to clamber over his shoulders.

"Where's all this going, then?" Sid popped the boot and reached in to grab a bag. "Jacinda had to make a stop, but she'll be here soon with the rest."

Davet froze at the sight of the bags. "I'd forgotten. Walking over here, I was happy. I forgot. I'm a horrible brother? How could I do that?"

"You're not—"

Davet darted by Sid, not wanting to hear comforting lies. He dropped Rabbit off in the room with the actual bunny. The two animals had been raised together by Fraco and despite being prey and predator tended to cuddle together happily.

Watching them for a while, Davet eventually turned

his attention to his grumbling stomach. He hadn't eaten much recently. With his parents in Bideford, he knew a clear mind was needed.

It always took a lot of strength and energy to handle them. He stood in the centre of the compact kitchen, staring blankly at the shiny surfaces. How did he get back to normal?

How the hell do I serve coffee with a smile and chat with everyone like always?

Davet hadn't managed to move towards the fridge to hunt for a suitable meal. He sank down to sit on the floor. "What am I going to do without him?"

"Survive." Fie stood behind him, squashed into the hallway with Sid. "You'll have days when even lifting your head from the pillow is too much to handle. And slowly, piece by piece, you'll manage to discover a way to carry on with your life."

"Food eventually stops tasting like dried arse," Sid added, grunting when Fie elbowed him in the stomach. "What? After I came back from war, everything I forced myself to eat was like rehydrated shit."

"Disgusting visuals aside, MacFluff has a point." Fie squeezed by Sid into the kitchen. He crouched down beside Davet, who couldn't bring himself to look at either man. "World won't be exactly the same, but you learn how to cope with the new version."

"How?" Davet didn't think he had the ability to be in a place without his brilliant and sweet little brother who'd seen the good in everyone, even the ugliest of animals. "How is that ever going to be possible?"

"You remember Fraco would want you to find joy again. And he'd want you to care for his miniature menagerie." Sid pushed Fie over and sat beside Davet. "Focus on all the good bits to get you through the awful ones."

"But, how?" Davet struggled to bring anything to mind other than a vision of Fraco's lifeless body face down in a dirty canal. "Did it work for you?"

"Some days." Fie seemed unmoved by Sid punching him lightly in the shoulder. "What? The truth is not everyone deals with grief the same. MacFluff handled mourning far easier than I did. And I'll be blunt. It took me years."

"Fair enough." Sid's blue eyes turned towards Davet. "For me, every year has been easier than the last. The happy memories outweigh everything else. I surrounded myself with photos as a reminder. They're still plastered all over my flat."

They made it sound so simple.

And so impossibly hard.

How do I survive through this awful nightmare to get to the days when life is slightly more tolerable?

Sid tapped Davet on the arm, drawing his attention. "You're not alone."

"You've a Fox that's a rabbit and a Rabbit who moonlights as a fox. You've also got this idiot. Me. Haggard, who'll probably do more good than anyone else. And the village. They all care about you," Fie offered. "And your uncle."

"I don't feel better." Davet wanted a magic wand to wave around to make him numb. He'd handled it better than the suffocating sadness.

"Give it time."

CHAPTER NINE

S<small>ID</small>

Over the course of his career first in the military and then as a police detective, Sid had dealt with a handful of grieving friends and family. This felt different. He wasn't sure why or how to shake off his strong desire to wrap Davet up in his arms to offer comfort.

Never wanted to wrap old Mrs Hardcastle up when her sister went missing.

They'd spent a few hours getting Davet settled, with Fraco's things mostly going into a spare room. Sid had hesitated to leave him alone, but duty called. His job was to investigate the death, not to hover over the living.

Sid was struggling with the investigation. Between getting coffee from Davet and helping Fraco with his strays, he'd grown close to the brothers. Jacinda had suggested passing on the case to another investigator; he couldn't.

Fraco deserved to have someone who cared working on it.

"You're too close." Jacinda wandered into his office, holding out a cup. "Made us some tea."

"Too close to what?" He accepted the tea with a grateful smile that broadened when she tossed him a packet of Jammie Dodgers. "Are we sharing?"

"Already had mine. Nicked these from the sergeant. Think she'll miss them?"

"Yes. And you're eating one of these so I have someone to share the blame with." Sid popped one into his mouth and held the packet out for her. "Well?"

"Don't talk with a full mouth." She grimaced.

"What am I too close to?" Sid swallowed a swig of tea to clear his throat.

"Fraco."

"Don't start again."

"I'm serious." Jacinda poked the stack of papers on his desk with the biscuit packet. "You're seeing villains in the shadows. The flatmates might be arrogant arseholes, but do you honestly believe they murdered Fraco? You read the coroner's report. He was drunk."

"Fraco didn't indulge in alcohol at all. He didn't even like fizzy drinks." Sid had questioned Santos about it, trying to avoid causing Davet any hurt. The uncle had insisted neither of them enjoyed any sort of liquor, not even beer. "So how did he get drunk?"

"What twenty-year-old doesn't get a bit tipsy once in their life?" Jacinda had a point, but he found it hard to believe of Fraco. "They didn't force-feed him beer, Sid."

"Fraco was a smart lad." Sid had always been amazed at the information he could rattle off about animals and agriculture. "Good with facts, figures, and books."

"And?"

"He was also naïve." He knew Santos had worried about both of his nephews; Fraco in particular, as Davet seemed to handle the non-autistic world far better than his brother. "How hard would it have been for those lads to trick him into getting drunk?"

"Sid."

"I'm serious." He couldn't shake the uneasiness about Fraco's flatmates. "It might not be murder, but they hold some responsibility if they got him drunk."

"And how will you prove it?" Jacinda's dark brown eyes speared him mercilessly. "Fraco may have decided to experiment. Lots of young adults do once out on their own. Peer pressure doesn't equate to manslaughter."

"It wouldn't be the first time." Sid knew from personal experience how dangerous the influence of friends at a young age could be. "We can't ignore the possibility. Did you find the flatmates a bit antsy around us?"

"We're coppers. You're taller than practically everyone I've ever met. Your friend Fie is more bear than man." Jacinda silenced his immediate instinct to crack a joke. "Don't say it. And I've already had the pleasure of cracking down on one of their parties."

"Oh. Right." Sid had read the report on the incident a few months back. The university students hadn't taken well to the police breaking up their fun—and showed it with quite a bit of antisocial behaviour including flinging racist slurs at Jacinda. She'd shown more restraint than Sid would've in her shoes. "Spoiled wankers."

"They are. I'm not sure they're killers." She grabbed another biscuit from the packet. "Still not sure why they thought I'd find Black-Hulk an insult. She-Hulk was a brilliant heroine."

"Nerd."

She lifted her new coffee mug that Fie had made custom for her with her new superhero moniker. "Careful or I'll crush you."

"I'm not ready to let the investigation go."

"The investigation or Fraco?"

Both.

Sid knew she had a point about his being too close to investigate. "I keep seeing him bringing in his reports of another animal being run over. He was such a sweet lad."

"He was." Jacinda stretched a hand across his messy desk to grab his. "Be there for Davet. But don't waste time on an investigation when there isn't one."

Sid shrugged. He would be there for Davet, despite the conflicting emotions that had begun to develop in the past few months. Another thing he'd gone out of his way to avoid. "Just a few more questions to answer and then I promise to close my case if I don't find anything."

"*Sidney.*"

Sid paused with the last Jammie Dodger halfway to his mouth. "You sounded suspiciously like my mum just then."

"Don't be a twat."

"Comes naturally to me." He jerked his hand out of hers when she pinched him. "*Oi.* You're assaulting an officer."

"I am an officer." She sat back in the chair. "This is why you need a partner. You run off all emotionally involved."

"Me?"

"Yes, you." Jacinda waved her hand towards the reports spread across his desk. "You always take cases like these personally."

"Right. Because we have so many deaths in Bideford." Sid spoke around the biscuit in his mouth. "Wouldn't you want your death looked into by someone who cared?"

They bickered good-naturedly for several more minutes before Jacinda returned to her own desk—and her actual partner. She had a point about Fraco's death. Sid just couldn't let the matter rest until his questions were answered.

For Fraco.

And for Davet if I'm honest with myself.

He stared at the report from the coroner until his eyes watered. "I'm going to ask Davet about his brother drinking."

Fuck a duck with a broken spork.

After two hours of wasting time, Sid ran out of emails to answer and reports to type up. He'd even managed to clear off his desk, putting away files from six months ago. Procrastination wasn't usually a problem he suffered from, but asking Davet about Fraco's drinking ranked up with some of the hardest conversations in his life.

Maybe not the most difficult; Sid reserved that spot for the time he'd come out to his father. Or maybe having to inform his best friend's family their daughter had been killed in the line of duty. He'd give his right arm to never go through conversations of that nature ever again.

Telling his father, a gruff, retired military man, that his only son was gay had gone about as well as Sid had thought it would. Unlike Fie's open-minded and loving parents, his dad hadn't bothered to hide his immense displeasure. They hadn't spoken since.

He often wondered if their next reunion would be at his father's grave. It hurt. His only blood relative in the world refused to speak to him.

Putting those painful thoughts to the side, Sid grabbed his keys and jacket to head out. The sooner questions were asked, the quicker his case could be closed. *One way or another.* Davet wouldn't thank him for putting off the inevitable.

"Sid?"

"Not it. You do the work, whatever it is." He continued out the door, leaving Jacinda's partner, Harry, to race after him. He lengthened his stride just to be irritating. "I'm in a hurry."

"Slow down, you bloody tree."

"Bloody tree? That honestly the best you can do?" Sid turned around when he reached his vehicle in the car park to grin at shorter Harry. "What sort of tree?"

"If you're finished being an annoying bastard?"

"I'm a mild irritant at best." Sid leaned against his vehicle.

"All the CCTV footage you wanted from along the road, cycling path, and the canal itself finally arrived. I've got it all on a thumb drive for you." Harry held it up for proof.

Sid glanced at his watch. Putting off the conversation with Davet would only make it harder. "Can you leave it on my desk for me? I've got questions for Fraco's family, and I'd rather not delay any further."

"Bring back coffee."

"Fine." Sid didn't know if Davet would be up for making their usual collection of drinks, not after the mildly crushing news he had to deliver. "I'll do my best."

Harry placed a hand on Sid's shoulder to stop him from getting into his vehicle. "Give him our best, yeah? Coffee First is the best coffee shop around.

He's a good lad. Always takes good care of us. Half the time we can't get him to let us pay for our drinks."

"Yeah."

"Want company?" Harry asked after Sid didn't move.

Yes.

"No, I've got it. Not the first time I've had to ask an acquaintance tough questions." Sid refrained from mentioning how much he wanted Davet to be more than an acquaintance. "Thanks."

"Sid?"

"Hmm?" He slid into the driver seat, glancing up at Harry. "What?"

"Don't get your heart broke, all right?"

"Tell Jacinda I'm going to pour glue in her keyboard." Sid slammed his door shut and sternly refused to allow himself to come close to blushing. "*Wankers.*"

CHAPTER TEN

DAVET

Despite his "closed for the week for bereavement" sign, Coffee First had a steady stream of visitors. His regulars dropped by with food, flowers, and kind offers of help. Their generosity overwhelmed him while also being a stark contrast to his parents, who'd harassed him at almost every opportunity.

His mother had shown up not long after Fie and Sid left. She'd wanted Fraco's things. Davet shut the door in her face.

Early the next day, his father had arrived. He'd pressed to come inside. Davet refused, and then dealt with them off and on until late in the evening.

This morning would likely be more of the same. Davet had an appointment with Father Sterling, Fraco's priest, to discuss the funeral. And he had no idea where to begin.

Though his brother had moved ten minutes away

from Bideford, Fraco had grown too attached to the Bideford parish to go anywhere. He usually made the trip for mass each week. Davet knew Father Sterling would be as kind and warm as always. The priest always came over for coffee after lunch.

In his two years of living in Bideford, Davet hadn't once stepped inside the church. Fraco had never pressed him to do so. They'd respected each other's decisions in life and belief.

And now in death.

Deciding to walk, Davet bundled up and made his way down the lane towards the church. He kept his head down, waving at anyone who greeted him without stopping. Father Sterling was changing the message on the board outside when he wandered up.

Father Sterling waved at him, then took his hand and patted it. "I'm so incredibly sorry to hear about Fraco. He spoke of you quite frequently. You were his favourite human."

"Fraco preferred animals to people." Davet stared down at their joined hands, unsure how to extract himself without being rude. He didn't want to offend the priest. "They didn't talk back to him."

Father Sterling let go of his hand and returned to finishing up with putting the letters onto the church board. "He'll be greatly missed. We had tea in the little garden we have every week. I'd find passages of scripture with animals for him, and he'd tend to our little bee colony. Your brother was a sweet lad who gave his whole heart to caring for the smallest of God's creation."

"Maybe your god should've spared a thought for caring for him?" Davet tried to bite back the words, but they came out anyway. "Isn't he a god of love and all that?"

"God has a plan."

Davet glanced up at the sky, letting the brisk breeze cool his temper. "Your god. And perhaps the plan was a bad one."

"Fraco—"

"I can't do this today." Davet spun around and jogged away from the church. He ran blindly without paying attention until he found himself standing outside of Fie's pottery workshop. "This is not home."

"Well spotted."

Davet glanced over to find Fie watching him from the doorway. "Hello."

"Any particular reason you chose to run in winter?"

"Philosophical differences with a priest." Davet sat on a stack of chopped wood with a groan. "I'm not ready to plan a funeral. But my parents will ruin the entire thing if I don't. They'll make a mockery of Fraco and what he loved—just because they can."

And they would. Davet knew the type of circus his mother called an event. Both of his parents would find reasons to make everything about them.

It had been a theme of his and Fraco's lives growing up, along with neglect.

And abuse.

Yet another reason why Davet could never understand Fraco's ability to find strength in a faith that had been used against them. He knew his parents had twisted the message. It was something he was never quite capable of forgiving either his mother and father or their god of love for.

"Davet?"

He blinked a few times and found Fie crouched in front of him. "Sorry?"

"I asked if you wanted to come inside for a cup of coffee. Not up to your standard, though if you prefer, I make a damn good hot chocolate." Fie rested a hand on the stack of wood beside where Davet sat. "Why don't you come into the cottage? Haggard and I were sitting down for an early lunch."

"Or late breakfast?"

"Had breakfast at four."

Davet could only stare at the man. Mostly at his nose to avoid eye contact. "Why?"

"Insomnia." Fie petted Haggard absently when the dog pressed up to his side. "Well? I'm freezing my arse off, so why don't we go inside. Haggard needs his mid-morning treat."

"And how many treats does he get?"

"You know the hobbits in Lord of the Rings? He's a combination of Merry and Pippin when it comes to food." Fie stood up then back to give Davet space. "Coming then? Grab a couple of those logs, would you."

Davet watched as Fie headed toward his front door. "Merde."

Stop thinking about him.
He's just being kind.
It doesn't mean anything.

Coffee had always been an art to Davet. He worked hard to ensure each mug was an experience. Fie appeared to be the same with hot chocolate.

He found himself sitting at a rough-hewn wooden table in the kitchen watching Fie concoct the magic. "How can you be incapable of making a decent cup of coffee but skilled with hot chocolate?"

"One of life's mysteries."

Davet blinked at Fie's back, trying not to get distracted by the broad shoulders. "So, like the Bermuda triangle but with cream?"

Ignoring him, Fie finished heating up the milk and added chocolate. Davet watched while he added cream and a tiny dash of cinnamon. He finished it off with a few dark chocolate shavings.

"Want to talk about it?"

"Fraco would've loved this." Davet clutched the mug in his hands tightly, allowing the warmth to soak into his skin. "I can't do this," he said after a moment.

"All of it? Or just the funeral?"

Davet both appreciated and hated Fie's constant refusal to be anything other than blunt. "How do I move forward without him?"

Fie drank some of his hot chocolate, reached back

into a kitchen drawer for a piece of paper, and slid it across the table to him along with a pen. "Jot down any task you believe you should have accomplished."

"Why?"

"Consider it the price of hot chocolate." Fie shrugged.

After glaring at the empty page, Davet wrote down whatever popped into his mind. *Donating Fraco's clothes, I can't wear them. Couldn't even if they fit. I should contact his university. And all the stuff in my cottage needs to be sorted. I've got to open the coffee shop.*

On paper, none of it seemed nearly as important as it had in his head.

Fie placed a plate with sandwiches on the table, leaning over to look at his list. "Put a star next to anything you have a deadline on that is out of your control."

"The funeral," Davet answered immediately. "Father Sterling has to know how to proceed."

Fie slid a second sheet of paper over to him. "In a perfect world, what would you want to honour your brother's memory?"

"I...." Davet didn't know what to write down. Seeing funeral plans on paper would make it final.

Which is probably his point.

"You can't save him." Fie sounded as though he spoke from personal experience. "All you can do now is keep your parents from taking over the funeral."

"Merde."

CHAPTER ELEVEN

Fie

Two nights of insomnia had given Fie a ton of time to research grief and how autistics dealt with loss, in between ignoring calls from Edmund, who couldn't take a hint. He'd struggled mostly on his own at the beginning, before his friends and loved ones intervened; Davet didn't need to suffer the same way. *Everyone handles mourning differently, but don't we all want someone to at least sit with us through the pain?*

Unless they're Sid, unfeeling git, who never shows any strain.

And now I sound like a bitter old bastard.

MacFluff's always been better with this shit. He's not the one labelled with a syndrome and saddled with a dog to keep him from going off the deep end.

Haggard huffed in his sleep, drawing Fie out of his thoughts.

He glanced down at Haggard, who had stretched

out on his side underneath the table. "Sorry. I'm not saddled with you."

Amidst all the negative, Haggard had been a brilliant light in the darkness. His bad days had slowly been growing easier to withstand. Fie thought hidden wounds might be the hardest to heal.

"Swayze? You up?" Sid knocked on the door.

Fie stood from the kitchen table and let his friend inside. "Up early, are we? Weren't you supposed to be meeting with Davet yesterday? He texted me to ask if I'd heard from you."

"I was." Sid leaned against the counter. "I've got some delicate questions for him, and I wanted to give myself time to consider."

"You chickened out." Fie moved over to top up his coffee and pour one for Sid. "Don't cock it up."

"Helpful, Swayze. Did I mention the questions were of a delicate nature? Why'd they make you a squad leader?" Sid teased.

Fie's stomach clenched painfully, as though Sid had kicked him in the gut. "I've no idea."

"Swayze." Sid reached out a hand towards him, pulling back when Fie waved him off. "Just a joke. You were the only person in the unit who could've brought us home."

"Not all of you. How many died in the blast?"

All those soldiers who trusted me with their lives, and I failed them.

"War is hell. You know this," Sid stated firmly.

"You could never have saved everyone, Fie. You went above and beyond the call of duty to save lives. I wouldn't fucking be here without you. So sod off with your bullshit guilt. You've got a George's Cross to prove it."

"Left the medal on Click's memorial." Fie hadn't believed his actions deserved an award, but his bomb-sniffing dog had certainly sacrificed his life to save lives. "We're not here to regurgitate the past."

"Maybe we should." Sid dragged one of the chairs away from the table to sit in, legs stretched out in front of him. "Might help."

"I've a therapist and a dog." Fie decided if they had to go over all of this, another rasher of bacon was required. "Want some?"

"Are you talking to Haggard or me?" Sid chuckled when the dog hopped immediately to his feet. "I could eat."

He popped a few slices of bread into the toaster and got to work on the bacon. "You're not usually here this early."

"Watson rang."

"*Bugger.*" Fie resisted the urge to bash his head against the cabinet. Watson, or Jane Freeman, was another former member of their squad who'd married Sherlock, or John. They'd earned their monikers from their obsession with a particular telly detective. "They're not driving over, are they?"

Jane and John trained service dogs for fellow veterans. They worked with several charities. Fie had them to thank for Haggard.

"Well?" Fie snapped when Sid simply grinned at him. "Did you bring them up for a reason? Or are you just being your normal aggravating self?"

"They're driving up for a visit. Sherlock's continuing on to London to deliver a new dog and Watson's decided to stick around here until he returns. Won't that be nice?" Sid joined him at the counter and started to butter the toast while Fie cracked a few eggs into a pan. "She wants to shop."

"Watson? She wants to shop? In Bideford?" Fie snorted in disbelief. "She hates going to the store even for groceries. What *did* you do?"

Sid focused intensely on the toast. "Nothing."

"Sidney." Fie scowled fiercely at one of his oldest friends. "Did you share something in particular during your last gossip session with the dog training duo?"

"We don't gossip. We chat. Friends stay in touch." He made it sound like a rebuke. "You might give it a try."

"I...." Fie hesitated, not sure he had an honest defence to offer. "I could do better."

"Hermits do better. People sending messages in a bottle do better," Sid snarked.

"I talk to Davet almost every morning." Fie focused his attention on the eggs, groaning internally and wishing he'd refused to open the door. "I email."

"We live ten minutes from each other." Sid placed a hand on Fie's shoulder. "We care."

"I know." Fie grabbed a couple of plates to get ready to dish up breakfast. "I think about reaching out. The phone even makes it to my hand. And then, I can't. A million reasons not to spring to my mind. Pressing Send on a call seems like climbing Mount Everest."

"We're not bill collectors. You don't have to duck our calls." He tossed the toast on the plates. "How many years have we known each other? I'm not a random stranger wanting to sell you biscuits or something."

"You don't understand." Fie gripped the spatula in his hand tightly. "I'm as irritable as a hungry bear on my bad days. Why bring everyone down by grumping at them?"

"Because we love you."

"Aren't we supposed to avoid all mentions of love?" Fie had blocked out their drunken admission and the one night that had followed. "It was your idea."

"Mine?" Sid pointed the butter knife at him. "I woke up, tangled in your bed, and you kicked me out on my arse. I had a hell of a hangover. Do you know how hard it is to walk to your car with dignity in nothing but a sheet?"

"I didn't want a pity fuck." Fie had been too drunk to really remember most of the night. "Still don't."

"You're a right arse."

"Can you be a wrong one?" Fie shoved a handful of bacon on both plates and added the perfectly fried eggs.

"Pedantic wanker." Sid grabbed the full plate and

moved over to one of the chairs. "Nothing pitiable about that night aside from my hangover and naked walk of shame."

"Gave you a sheet."

"Gave? You were too sodding hungover to volunteer your bed linens." Sid flicked a piece of bacon under the table towards Haggard, who practically inhaled it. "Aren't you lonely?"

"No."

Yes.

"Sure." Sid stared in obvious disbelief at Fie. "Would you rather I talk about something else?"

"Yes."

"Fraco had a massive amount of alcohol in his system."

"What?" Fie narrowly managed to avoid spitting out the bacon in his mouth. "Fraco? The kid never drank."

"I know."

"And now you have to ask Davet?" Fie didn't envy him having to start that conversation. "I'll come with you. After breakfast."

And maybe we can shelve the conversation about the night that shall not be named and everything else connected with it forever.

CHAPTER TWELVE

Davet

"What are you doing?" Davet yanked the coffee mugs out of his mother's hand to return them to their shelf. "Will you just get out of my cottage? You're messing up my shop."

"Silly idiot." She waved a hand dismissively at him and returned to where she'd been pulling custom mugs out of a kitchen cabinet. "You've done this all wrong. What were you thinking? Oh, of course, you're not quite capable of *processing* the world, are you?"

Davet twisted away from her, gritting his teeth and trying to put words together to express his wish for her to leave. He tried to shut the cabinets but didn't want to hurt her. *Not that she gives a shit about hurting me. Never has, likely never will.*

The battle with his parents began at the church, which, given his experiences as a child, had a certain amount of twisted irony. He'd braved the second meeting with Father Sterling. It had gone far better than the first—until his parents swanned in wanting to take over and change all the carefully made plans.

To his surprise, Father Sterling had politely but sternly excluded them from the discussion. He told Davet how Fraco had spoken in depth about their traumatic childhood. The priest refused to allow the abuse to continue after death; Fraco wouldn't have wanted either their mother or father to be involved at all.

Leaving the sanctuary, Davet found his parents waiting for him. He practically jogged home to avoid them, ignoring how the bitterly cold air burned with each breath. They still managed to follow close behind.

His day had continued to descend into an all too familiar nightmare. Davet struggled to verbalise that he didn't want them in his home—his safe space. They pressed inside anyway, attempting to take control.

Frustration ate at him.

Why can't I just find the words to tell them off when I really need to?

I hate my brain.

No, I don't.

But I do. Today, today at least.

Grabbing his phone, Davet texted his Uncle Santos, who immediately promised to come over after work. *What do I do until then? Aside from losing what's left of my mind?*

A screech down the hall drew his attention. Davet raced over to find his father holding Fox by the scruff of the neck while Rabbit cowered in the corner. Rage bubbled up inside of him instantly.

"Give me the rabbit. *Now*." Davet gently plucked the trembling animal out of his father's hands. "Get out of my cottage. And take your wife with you. Get. Out."

"Who do you think you're talking to?" His father began shouting at him rapidly in French, looming over him with his fists clenched.

"An ignorant, abusive bully who hasn't learned anything since the court intervened in our lives." Davet stuck with English to annoy him. "If you don't leave, I'll call the police."

Before further words could be exchanged, a knock rattled his back door. Davet slipped by his father with the rabbit in his arms and his brother's fox following on his heels. They went down the hall to see who had brought the welcome interruption.

"Hello?"

Davet blinked a few times in an attempt to process the sudden appearance of both Sid and Fie. "Did Uncle Santos send you?"

"No." Sid shook his head before narrowing his eyes. "Why? What's wrong?"

"An invasion of sorts." Davet glanced over his shoulder when his parents started arguing with each other loudly—in French and English. "They won't leave."

Sid exchanged a look with Fie, who nodded, clearly understanding something that had gone over

Davet's head. "Why don't you and Swayze stay here with the fox-rabbit and the rabbit-fox? I'll flash my badge and handle your invaders."

"MacFluff has a lot of experience shutting down arseholes," Fie promised. "How've you been?"

"Fine." Davet moved over to sit on a large rock behind the cottage. He shivered in the cold air, regretting his decision to step outside. "Terrible."

"Here." Fie pulled off his coat to offer it.

Davet shoved it away with one hand while clutching Fox to his chest. "I'll be fine."

"You'll be hypothermic." He eased back into his coat and apparently decided not to force the issue. "How'd it go with the vicar?"

"Priest."

"Is there a difference?"

Davet had no idea. He'd blocked out all the religious knowledge his parents had shoved into their brains as children. "Probably."

Their lazy debate trailed off as his parents stormed past them. Sid appeared seconds later, a wide smirk on his face. Davet turned away from the man, unsure how to handle the sudden warmth in his body.

"Are you two coming inside?" Sid asked with a laugh.

Davet bent down to lift up Rabbit. He carried both animals inside, staring at Sid's back. That laugh had sounded a bit forced. "Why are you here?"

When neither man responded, Davet decided to

wait them out. He settled Fox and Rabbit in their room and closed the door. Sid and Fie followed him into the kitchen, where he could only stare in horror at the chaos his mother had brought to his workspace.

The mugs for his regulars, usually kept lined up on one of the counters, had all disappeared. Davet grimaced at the coffee beans scattered on the floor. He wondered if she'd been moving one of the many bags of coffee when Sid chased them out of the house.

Muttering angrily to himself in French, Davet dealt with the messiest issue first, the coffee beans. He grabbed the small dustpan and miniature broom kept in the kitchen for accidental spills. When Fie moved to help him, Davet waved him off with a scowl; his comfortable space had been ruined and wouldn't feel the same until he fixed it.

"Let us help." Sid broke the silence after watching Davet on his hands and knees sweeping up the tiny coffee beans. "What can we do?"

"Leave me alone." Davet didn't know if he could handle another minute in his favourite place in the cottage, his kitchen, messed up because of his mother. "I will fix this. I will. You can't, so just let me reorder my world."

To his surprise, Sid and Fie retreated to the opposite side of the room to sit at his tiny table. They chatted quietly with each other, leaving him with a semblance of privacy. Davet switched on his radio to drown out their conversation and continued sweeping up the coffee.

After stowing the pan and brush under the sink, Davet stared blankly at the mugs for a moment. He rubbed his hands on his trousers, trying to get rid of the itchy sensation on his palms. *Why is this so hard? I know where they go; I should be able to put them back in the cabinet.*

He stared.

And stared.

And stared.

Merde.

"Davet?"

He scratched at his palms again. "It's all wrong."

Fie moved out of his chair to stand near him, not crowding too closely. "Can we help?"

Davet didn't honestly know how to answer, or if he could answer for that matter. He grabbed one of the mugs for something to do with his hands. "I have to fix it."

"Okay." Fie nodded. Haggard stretched out on the floor by the front door, keeping out of the way but obviously watching his human. "How about you take a few breaths? Yeah? Count out the seconds for me; focus on the numbers for a bit. Just in and out."

Counting had never worked for Davet. Fraco had been endlessly fascinated by counting, particularly in different languages. He'd made songs out of the numbers.

With the off-key melody in his mind, Davet counted to ten in a few languages. Fraco had sung them so many times that he'd memorised them himself. The happy memory helped more than the actual breathing or numbers.

"Oi. Swayze. When did you become a Zen master?" Sid flicked a stray coffee bean toward Fie. "How'd you know the breathing trick would work?"

"Not sure it did." Fie batted away the bean.

"Mugs." Davet found once his mind cleared that he had a far better grasp on what to do next. He suddenly remembered a note on his fridge to ask Fie about new ones. "Did I email you the order to replace the broken cups?"

"You did." Fie nodded sharply. "I'd already started to work on them. I should have a box of mugs for you by the end of the week."

Muttering a short thank-you, Davet began reorganising his cabinets. He managed to return everything to normal quickly. With the last mug set in its spot, he found himself wondering why the two men had shown up at all.

"So, why are you here?" He turned around to find Fie and Sid exchanging a look. "What? Quit with the facial expressions I can't interpret."

"Why don't you sit?"

"Because if I'm getting bad news, I'd rather be over here in my own personal bubble." Davet scowled at Sid, who'd reached out to pat one of the empty chairs.

Sid scratched his jaw for a minute. "Are you sure you don't want to sit down?"

"Quite sure." Davet didn't believe any news could be worse than hearing his brother had died. "Well?"

CHAPTER THIRTEEN

Sid

Talking about Fraco's inebriated state at the time of his death hadn't exactly gone well. Eventually, Davet had covered his ears and stormed out of the room. A door slammed a few seconds later, and Sid stared helplessly at a bemused Fie.

"A-plus interrogation skills, MacFluff. You handled that delicate situation with all the finesse of a baby giraffe on an ice skating rink." Fie took their coffee mugs to the sink and began washing them. "Did you sleep through training on speaking with bereaved family members?"

"Not actually helpful, Swayze. Less sarcasm, more encouragement." Sid grabbed a tea towel, rolled it, and flicked Fie on the arse. "Should I go talk to him or wait until he comes back?"

"Maybe with a tiny amount of tact." Fie smirked over his shoulder at him.

The smile briefly reminded Sid of the jovial jokester of a man Fie had been before war. Grief changed everyone. As their leader, Fie had believed life and death had rested in his hands.

Egotistical wanker.

As though none of us knew the dangers before we left?

They'd all known the hazards of being in a bomb detection unit. Afghanistan had been an environment where losing someone had been all but guaranteed. They'd all gone anyway, in the hopes of using their skills to save lives.

Sid knew without a doubt their fallen family members would've held no anger towards Fie. He wished a magic wand existed to take away the pain. It hurt to watch him continually struggle. "Fie."

He twisted around from the sink to face Sid. "You're about to be an emotional MacFluff about something."

"I could shove your face into the soapy water." Sid found the lump in his throat vanished instantly with his slight exasperation. The *new* Fie generally dodged any conversation that might involve emotions. "We didn't all die in the blast, Swayze. I'm here. Why can't you ever just fucking let us care about you? Maybe I want to celebrate being alive. We all came back with scars, man. Why won't you let us heal together?"

"Sexual healing?"

"Would it help?" Sid could play the avoidance game as long as necessary if Fie eventually managed to face up to things.

"Are you two a couple?" Davet seemed surprisingly crestfallen at the idea. He hesitated before stepping fully into the kitchen. "I shouldn't have stormed off like a child. I'm sorry. I'll hear you out."

"First, we're not a couple." Sid kept his eyes on Fie while answering. His old friend's eyes narrowed. *How fascinating.* "Second, no apologies necessary. This isn't a topic I wanted to bring up with you, but I have to get to the bottom of this if you want answers to what happened to Fraco."

"He didn't drink. Not even wine at church. The priest substituted grape juice just for him," Davet insisted. "He'd never be drunk. Ever. I don't understand. Could it be a mistake?"

"No." Sid thought honesty would be better for Davet in the long run. "Is it possible he decided to have a beer with his friends at university? If he'd never had alcohol before, he might not have noticed the effects until it was too late."

"No." Davet had already started shaking his head vigorously before Sid finished speaking. "Never. He didn't even like fizzy drinks or anything bitter. He wouldn't have voluntarily gotten so inebriated he passed out in a river."

Which led to the obvious question, did Fraco involuntarily get drunk? How hard would it have been for someone to trick the young autistic into a first alcoholic beverage? And after one, more might easily have followed.

"All right, all right." Sid raised his hands as Davet became increasingly upset. He didn't want him storming off again. "Who did Fraco spend time with? His roommates? Other classmates?"

"His animals." Davet shrugged. He scrubbed his fingers across his face roughly. "Fraco didn't make friends easily. Not that I do either. He sometimes got dragged along with his roommates because he struggled with knowing how to say no."

His cynical detective side told him Fraco had likely decided to rebel. Away from any parental figure, Davet had definitely been more father than their sperm donor. They'd been raised with a zealous religious background, and he'd found faith once free from restrictions. Was it beyond the realm of possibility that he'd gone a bit wild?

It wouldn't be the first time a child had grown up in a repressed home only to spin out of control as an adult.

"He didn't drink," Davet insisted confidently. "Ever. He was afraid to feel out of control."

If that's true, I'm going to need to revisit his roommates.

In the end, the conversation with Davet had left Sid with more questions than answers. Fie motioned toward the door, and Sid wrapped up the conversation. They weren't getting anywhere pestering him about Fraco.

While Fie returned to his kiln to work on mugs, Sid made the drive to Fraco's former flat. He repeatedly knocked on the door. *No answer*. He had no doubt they were inside, given the fact the curtains had moved as he drove up.

What now?

I wonder if their professors will have anything to add to the conversation.

Can't hurt, can it?

CHAPTER FOURTEEN

FIE

As much as Fie wanted to stay for Davet, he knew they had to give him space to process. The world had dumped a lot on his shoulders in the short space of a week. They could be there for him by stepping away.

And maybe I'll find the time to deal with the honesty Sid verbally flayed me with.

Two hours of sweating in his workshop by the kiln wore him out in the best way. Fie usually found his mind clearer and the strain of guilt easier to bear after the physical labour of finishing up an order. He stepped outside with Haggard on his heels to let the crisp winter air cool him off.

"Fetch, is it?" Fie glanced down when Haggard hit him on the leg with the stick in his mouth. "Ready to do a bit of running?"

Grabbing the stick, Fie threw it across the empty field that served as his garden. He'd wanted space—

not flowers. Haggard trotted back over to him and dropped his prize at Fie's feet, glancing up expectantly.

"If you could master the throwing and the fetching, I'd give you a steak for breakfast, lunch, and dinner." Fie launched the stick into the distance. "Silly mutt."

"Talking to yourself again, Swayze?"

Fie glanced over to find Jane Freeman sitting on the nearby fence. "Watson. Where's your Sherlock?"

"Already on the way to London. We left home a bit late, so he didn't have time to hang around. He'll have plenty of time on his way back, though." She smiled brightly at him, hopping down. "How've you been?"

Fie turned away to stare at Haggard, who was racing from one side of the garden to the other. He found it hard at times to look at Jane. She was a beautiful black woman, but all he saw was the bloody body he pulled from the wreckage of their vehicle after the blast. He'd done everything in his power to save her life. "I'm fine."

"Fine for Fie can mean anything from I'm a minute away from drowning myself to I'm as happy as Haggard with crispy bacon." She wandered over to stand beside him, chuckling when his service dog greeted her with his stick. "Men and their wood."

"*Jane.*"

"Yes?" She smiled brightly at him before throwing Haggard's stick. "I'm not bleeding anymore—aside from once a month when the universe tests my temper and need for chocolate. I lived. You saved me, and

John, and so many others. I'll repeat that over and over until you eventually believe me."

Fie wanted to tell her not to bother. How many years had he struggled with the monster of grief? "I'm getting better."

"I know, love. You've definitely improved from the days when you sat in your dark, cold cottage ignoring our knocking at the door." Jane sidled up next to him and rested her head against his shoulder. She stood almost as tall as him. "We want to see you happy."

"Did my mum send you?"

Jane snickered at him, shoving away from him when Haggard trotted over again with his prize. "She texts me twice a day. Once about you. And once about my dogs."

"Never about you or John?" Fie dragged a hand across his face tiredly. His mum had a two-track mind at times. "Sorry, Watson. I'll talk to her."

"Don't. It's lovely. She sends homemade biscuits for our puppies. And she knits sweaters for them in the winter." Jane sent the stick flying for a happy Haggard, who practically launched himself across the field after it. "We natter for at least an hour on the phone every week. I talk to your mum more than I talk to my own."

"Should I be worried, horrified, or pleased for you?" Fie had no idea his mum kept in such close contact with his friends. "Does she call Sid?"

"Of course."

Fie definitely went from bemused to slightly horrified. "I have no words."

"Yes, you do. Invite me in for tea and biscuits. I'm starving." Jane whistled for Haggard, who came faster for her than he did for Fie. "Well? Are we going inside or not?"

"Have you ever wondered why you weren't commanding officer?" Fie had always thought she'd have managed better than he with the pressure.

"Daily." Jane shoved him towards the door. "I wouldn't have saved everyone. So get that thought out of your head. You didn't bloody fail us."

"I know."

"Very convincing." She dodged by him once inside to head over to fill the kettle with water. "I'm making the tea. You let it stew for too long."

"Don't."

"Yes, you do. You're worse than my John." Jane got the kettle going and twisted around towards him. "Now, what's this I hear about you and a certain young barista?"

"You hear nothing."

"I'm not Colonel Klink," she retorted.

"What?" Fie stared at her in bewilderment. "Who?"

"Never mind. Obscure reference. My nan loved old American shows on the telly." Jane grabbed his box of tea and two mugs. He refused to use cups; they usually felt too fragile for his hands. "Well? How is Davet doing? Still adorably handsome and skittish?"

"He's not skittish. Or adorable. He *is* attractive. And way too young for a damaged old soldier." Fie internally grumbled at himself. Jane had a habit of getting honest responses from him when he'd be more likely to tell Sid or John to bugger off with their questions. "Just play the mother."

"I'll mother you upside your head with the kettle." She waved one of the mugs threateningly at him. "You'd make the sweetest couple. Or maybe a trio with Sidney?"

Fie choked on his own saliva, glaring at her impish grin. "Please stop."

"Think about it."

That's all I'll be bloody doing now that you've put it in my mind.

"And no, I don't mean think about the porn-tastic possibilities." She tapped her fingers on the counter while waiting for the kettle to boil.

"Porn-tastic isn't a word." Fie willed away the definitely less than pure thoughts in his mind. "I've some sort of cake if you want a slice."

"Some sort of cake? I'm filled with confidence on the quality." She peeked inside the counter. "Is that the lemon and blueberry drizzle cake from the Old Bakery?"

"It is." Fie moved over to grab plates and a knife. "And no, Watson, you can't eat what's left. I'm having a slice as well."

"You're such a selfish git." Jane grabbed the kettle when it whistled piercingly to pour it into the teapot. "You need a new one."

"Teapot works."

"The handle is gone, the side is chipped, and you barely have a lid." She lifted it up, moving it to swirl around the liquid inside. "Why don't you buy a new one?"

"I like mine." Fie had gotten the teapot from one of their fallen comrades. "Jane? Leave it, please?"

She narrowed her eyes on him, watching for a minute before shrugging. Haggard trotted over with his mouth dripping water from having drunk out of his dish. He collapsed dramatically under the table with a whine.

"Ever the comedian." Fie grabbed the jar with the dog biscuits from his mum to throw one over to Haggard. "We're not discussing Davet. Or Sid. Or your dirty mind."

"Spoilsport."

"Do you want cake or not?"

"Fine." She swirled the tea a few more times before beginning to fill their mugs. "I'll leave it for now. We're going to have a chat about your inability to see the path to sexual pleasure and happiness."

"Did John send you on a wellness retreat again?" Fie remembered the last time Jane had been unpleasantly surprised with a forced holiday for her birthday. She had gone out of the way to torment all of them with all the buzzwords crammed down her throat.

"No. He's learnt his lesson." She slid his mug over for him to fix up while she measured out sugar for herself.

"On the plus side, we did determine the best way to help me relax was not a meditation clinic."

"How long was he on the couch?" Fie grabbed a chunk of cake along with his mug and sat at the kitchen table. "Actually, never mind, why the hell are you here?"

"Let's talk about sex—"

Fie stretched his arm across the table, grabbed her slice of cake, and shoved it into his mouth. He scowled while chewing. "How about no."

"You're a thieving bastard." She snatched his plate from him. "Are you going for celibacy?"

"I will give you the entire cake if you'll stop."

"I'll take the cake, and you'll answer my question." She pointed her spoon at him. "You're alive, Fie. Alive. At some point, you're going to have to start acting like you realise it."

"I know."

"Do you?" Jane canted her head to the side, staring at him intently enough he almost wanted to fidget. "Then what's the holdup?"

"He's young. He's grieving. And I'm not going to be that arsehole who takes advantage of him." Fie angrily chomped on a bite of cake, disintegrating it in his mouth. "He probably thinks I'm far too old for him."

"He stares at your arse. A lot."

"How would you know?"

"I have my sources." Jane grinned brightly before

sipping her tea.

"Sid gossips worse than anyone I've ever met," Fie grumbled.

"MacFluff wasn't my source." She waved off his prodding for more information. "Maybe your coffee man needs a distraction from all the terrible chaos around him?"

"No." Fie refused to approach Davet in any manner other than simply as a friend during his overwhelming grief. "I'm done with this conversation."

CHAPTER FIFTEEN

Davet

"Davet? Are you in here, son?" Uncle Santos's voice carried through the cottage. He'd kept a spare key to the place in case of emergency. "Can we talk? Please? Your auntie dragged your mum and dad off for the day so they won't be around to harass you."

Davet pulled the blankets off his head, lifted Fox and Rabbit out of his lap to get them settled, and got slowly to his feet. He'd ignored everyone for the past twenty-four hours. "They'll be back. The funeral is tomorrow. You know they're going to make a scene."

Tripping over one of Rabbit's toys, Davet made it into the hallway to find his uncle waiting for him. He waved absently at the man. Whatever Santos wanted to talk to him about, coffee would definitely be required.

His uncle followed him into the kitchen, watching him move woodenly over to make coffee for them and breakfast for himself. "We've no real reason to legally force them to leave."

"And yet, you welcomed them into your home." Davet loved his uncle deeply, but it hurt when no one in their family had actually spoken out against his parents' behaviour. "You're not Switzerland. I had to fight for Fraco alone. You gave us a safe place afterwards, and I'm grateful. I'll never understand, why didn't anyone try to help us earlier?"

"We had no tangible proof strong enough to make a custody fight across countries winnable." Uncle Santos reached out to grab Davet into a hug. He didn't hold on when Davet ducked away. "I'm sorrier than you'll ever know that we failed to protect both of you as children."

"We were worth the fight." Davet found forgiving and forgetting hard to do, particularly for the two hurt little boys who'd suffered for so long with no end in sight. But he didn't have the energy to argue, not with the funeral coming up. "Coffee or tea?"

Uncle Santos seemed to consider his words carefully before shrugging. "Coffee. You don't have to forgive me, son."

"I know." Davet grabbed the smaller of his French presses. "I love you, Uncle Santos. Fraco forgave you. Catholics are big on forgiveness."

"I miss him."

Davet breathed through the sudden anger and despair; Fraco had always urged him to forgive their uncle. He would try for his baby brother's sake—in his memory. "I miss him so much that my chest hurts and my throat clogs up. I can't breathe. I barely sleep. All I think about is how confused, scared, and cold Fraco must've been. And alone. He drowned in the dark, freezing water. Without me. Without anyone."

"I know." Tears flowed freely down his uncle's cheeks. "I know, son."

"I'm so angry. Whatever this feeling is…. I'm angry." Davet slammed the French press on the edge of the counter and dropped to his knees, choking on painful sobs. "Why wasn't I there?"

"It's not your fault, Davet. Tragic accidents can happen to anyone, even the sweetest and gentlest souls in the world." Santos crouched in front of him. "You weren't meant to be there."

"Meant? Who decided?"

Shoving his uncle's hands away, Davet got to his feet. He checked on Fraco's animals, grabbed his jacket, and left the cottage. The cold air snatched away the little breath he could manage while walking. He rested heavily on a fallen stump, surprised at how far his shaky legs had carried him—straight to Fie's door.

Again.

"Well, you look completely done in."

Davet glanced up and stared at the small scar between Jane's eyes. He'd met her a few times when Sid brought her by the coffee shop. "Yes."

"Want to talk about your troubles?" She walked over from the door to sit on a second stump nearby. "I'm quite good at playing agony aunt."

Davet shrugged.

"Want me to bugger off and leave you to the brisk breeze to think by yourself?" She didn't sound as though she'd be upset if he said yes. "There's hot coffee inside. Not as good as yours, but I made it since Fie tends to create a bizarre swill strong enough to stunt your growth and put hair on your chest."

"How does coffee stunt your growth?" Davet stared at her in confusion.

Jane shook her head with a wry chuckle. "Fie makes toxic sludge for coffee."

"Okay." Davet thought she might be teasing him, but sometimes he found allistics hard to read. *Sometimes? They're always so strange.* "I'm angry."

"Are you?"

"Yes." Davet dug his fingers into his knees, rocking slightly on the stump. "At my parents for being here. At Uncle Santos for not sending them off. At Fraco for dying. And for drinking, if he did. At everyone for saying they know how I must be feeling when they couldn't possibly understand."

And at myself, because I should've saved him.
And for not understanding how I'm feeling.
Stupid. So stupid.

Jane reached out tentatively to lay her hand on his clenched fist. "Whatever you're thinking about yourself isn't true at all. Most people throw clichéd words of comfort because they don't know how to help someone who's grieving."

"And you do?" Davet couldn't stop his voice from sounding bitter and brittle.

"Fie, me, and Sid. Between the three of us, we've been where you have. Lost people we loved more than life itself. Kills you inside. Eats you up, thinking maybe if you'd done one thing differently, everyone would've come home alive." She smiled sadly then, patting his hand and sitting back. "Training dogs is my penance, you see. We teach them to help our uniformed family that comes back haunted and wounded."

"Does it make you feel better?" Davet asked desperately.

"Most days." Jane breathed in quite deeply, shivering in the cold air. "The first step is realising you're never going to be able to change what's already happened."

"How does that help?"

"Well, if you can't change the past, you can make decisions about what comes next." She reached out slowly to unfurl his fingers. "Nothing you do now will bring your lovely brother back to us, but we can honour his memory. What do you suggest?"

"Planned the funeral already."

"And? Is it Fraco-esque enough?" Jane asked.

"Yes. No." Davet shook his head, then got to his feet to pace in front of her, which usually helped him think. "Father Sterling didn't think we should have animals in the church."

"Then bring Father Sterling to Fraco's animals." Her immediate response made Davet glance over to see if she was making fun of him. "I'm serious. I didn't know your brother as well as Sid or Fie. They've told me so many stories about him and his creatures. He had his faith as well. If your priest won't bring the animals to his god, then bring him to them instead."

"Not very traditional."

"Are you very traditional?" Jane seemed quite adamant about her idea. "Was Fraco?"

Davet pondered her questions for a while in silence. He'd done his best to compromise between what he assumed people expected and a memorial Fraco would've appreciated. "I don't know how to do this right."

"Can I help?" She reached out to try to grab his hand. "I'm a bit brilliant at planning."

"I don't know."

"She's had practice with planning memorials." Fie wandered around the side of the cottage with his arms full of firewood, Haggard faithfully trotting along at his side. Even with his depressed mood, Davet practically devoured the image Fie made; it was like the calendar his uncle had given him as a joke for Christmas. "Fraco loved the beach at Peppercombe and the walk through the valley to it. Why not see if the priest is up for a wander through the fields?"

"Not sure everyone will enjoy freezing on a hike for a memorial." Davet thought Fraco would've loved a homily in nature.

"Then they don't need to be there," Jane stated firmly. "And we'll be sure to squash any complaints. The day is about your brother—and you. End of story. Not about anyone else. If your priest doesn't cooperate, I'm sure we can find one who isn't so precious about where prayer happens."

"He's a nice man." Davet had no idea why he felt the need to defend Father Sterling. He hadn't warmed to the man, though the priest had been perfectly nice. Trusting people of faith didn't come naturally to him. "What if he says no?"

"Tell you what." Jane hopped up to her feet and waved him towards Fie's cottage. "It's rather nippy out here. Why don't we go inside? You can make coffee that doesn't taste like swill from a farmer's bucket, and we'll come up with a plan of action."

"Say yes. She'll only badger us until you do." Fie smiled at him, and Davet had the strangest sensation of melting into a puddle on the ground. He didn't, thankfully, but he blushed when Jane snickered at him. "Stop terrifying him, Watson. It's rude."

Jane snapped a salute, then winked at Davet. "Always let him think he's in control. Makes it easier to yank the rug out from under him."

"Why would I want to yank a rug out from under him?" Davet followed them hesitantly towards the steps. "He's standing on the ground, not a carpet."

"I…." Jane didn't appear to have a retort for him.

"He has a point. I am not actually standing on carpet." Fie sounded amused to Davet, but he was never sure. "Are we going inside?"

CHAPTER SIXTEEN

Sid

Jane: Bully the priest into an outdoor funeral for Fraco via a walk to Pennecombe. Or rather, bully him into agreeing when Davet asks.

Sid closed and opened his eyes, but the bewildering text message remained the same. "Bully the priest? Is that a euphemism?"

Why am I talking to myself? Arguing with Jane never ended well; she usually won. *How am I supposed to bully Father Sterling?*

With a tired sigh, Sid massaged his forehead to ease the sudden onset of the special brand of headache Jane always brought with her own brand of chaos. Organised and demanding chaos. She always managed to manoeuvre the world around to her liking.

He loved her for it, especially when she'd worked miracles with Fie. Her refusal to give up had driven their friend to finally accept help. And Haggard. Sid knew both Jane and John had worked especially hard to provide the perfect service animal for him.

Sid almost dropped his phone when it buzzed in his hand with another message. "Am I there yet? You just.... For fuck's sake."

Patience didn't come naturally to Jane. Not always. Sid had always thought it had been her one flaw that kept her from having command of her own unit. Aside from Fie, none of them had been suited for a leadership role.

Sid scrolled up and dialled Jane's number. She answered on the second ring with a crisp greeting. "What exactly am I bullying Father Sterling into doing for Davet?"

"Changing the funeral plans." Jane muttered something away from the phone before returning to him. "A wilderness walk to celebrate Fraco's life."

"In winter? What if it snows again?" Sid didn't know how willing the priest would be to step so far outside of the usual. "Fraco did enjoy all the trails around Devon."

And the animals.

Mostly the animals.

"The funeral should be about Fraco." Jane sounded as though she were walking out of the cottage. "What would he have wanted?"

"To be alive." Sid had never agreed completely with Jane's thoughts on memorials. "Funerals are for the living, Watson. Fraco is beyond caring. I imagine he'd be pleased and anxious about a group of people gathering in his name. He didn't like crowds."

"Don't be so cold," she reproved. "I thought you cared about Davet. This matters to him, Sidney."

"I do care." Sid refused to take the bait in the hint of a tease he heard in her voice at his caring about Davet. "If he wants a funeral hike, I'm in. I don't believe he needs any added pressure on creating a perfect memorial for Fraco, kind soul that he was, when his brother is beyond awareness. Fraco's dead. He can't appreciate any of this. How can we help Davet? He's my focus, Watson. If walking through the brambles eases his pain, let's make it happen."

"Funerals are a way of—"

Sid cut her off with a frustrated huff. "Jane. Can we not do this again? I love you, Watson. I'm not bickering with you."

"Callous bastard."

"I'm not, and you know it. I care deeply about Davet." Sid had felt the same about Fraco as well. *Maybe not exactly the same.* "We don't all grieve the same way."

"You don't."

Sid inhaled sharply. "You're narking up the wrong tree. You know I grieve deeply in my own way. I'm just not prone to dwelling on pain. I'll chat with Father Sterling."

"MacFluff."

"Just because I don't sob into my pillow endlessly doesn't mean I didn't grieve in my own way." Sid didn't want Jane to bulldoze her way over Davet, who might not have the capacity to say no. "Is this honestly what Davet wants?"

"Of course."

"Watson."

"I promise I only asked him what he thought his brother would've wanted," Jane insisted. "And off topic, you'll be thrilled to know Fie actually blushed when I brought up that the three of you would be excellent together."

"You didn't."

"Must go. Bye." Jane ended the call quickly.

Bugger.

After sending a text to Jane to tell her to leave Fie alone, Sid continued on his way to Fraco's old flat. He'd finally gotten the roommates to respond to his calls. They'd given him the run around for a while until they realised he had no intention of going away without having all of his questions answered.

Honest answers, not the bullshit they'd told at first. Sid thought they'd held something back. He didn't know if there'd been malicious intent behind those lies, but their story made no sense.

As a non-drinker, Fraco wouldn't have guzzled down such a substantial amount of booze alone. Once drunk, how had he gotten out to the canal on his own without being seen? Doubtful. Sid had begun to consider the idea that the tragic night had begun as a badly advised prank.

Let's get the autistic drunk and see what he does.

With years of experience dealing with what Jane called "laditude," Sid bought the idea of a cruel prank going wrong. He had no doubts they were capable of such juvenile behaviour. Fraco would've been easy prey for those sorts of tricks.

Heading up to the flat, Sid knocked impatiently on the door. *No answer. The little shitheads.* He waited a few minutes, banging periodically with no results. Several calls to them were also ignored.

Right.

That's not suspicious at all, bunking off on a meeting with a detective.

A few more calls got him in contact with the property manager, who told him the group had vacated in the middle of the night. They'd left a note on top of a box by the door. She readily handed both over to Sid, who discovered the items inside belonged to Fraco.

Sid deposited the box inside his boot and called Jacinda. "Fraco's flatmates moved out in the middle of the night with no forwarding address."

"Sid."

"You don't find it strange at all?"

"I find you strange." Jacinda sounded resigned. "Since I know you won't let anything go, I'll see if we can trace where they went."

"Thank you, Jacinda. You're a gem. A diamond

amongst a bucket of charcoal." Sid made a mental note to bring her a bribe of cake.

"In a bucket of charcoal?"

"I ran out of ideas." Sid shrugged. "Anything else? I've got to see a priest about a hike."

"I'm not asking."

"Good." Sid adjusted his mental note to get an entire cake, not just a slice. "Want a coffee?"

"Bribery will get you everywhere."

CHAPTER SEVENTEEN

Fie

It was a beautiful day for a funeral, particularly considering their typical January weather. Jane had managed to organise everyone in her usual manner. They gathered at the Bucks Mill car park to begin their walk.

Fie watched with concern as Davet fidgeted on the edge of the group. He wandered over with Haggard at his heels to check on him. "I know you're not okay, but can I help?"

"No."

"I brought a cuddly toy." Sid held out a fox to Davet. "Fraco left this in my back seat once during one of his rescues. I've meant to return him to you. Hoped you might feel his presence more with it."

"I'm supposed to lead everyone." Davet clutched the fox to his chest. "Jane suggested—"

"Jane's a lovely lunatic who isn't always right but

usually comes from a place of kindness." Fie stepped in before Sid could voice his thoughts on the subject. "What if MacFluff and I go with you?"

So they did.

Their procession meandered along a winding path through the woods to the shoreline. Though cold, the wind had died down enough to make the hike seem almost pleasant. Father Sterling went ahead of them with an incense holder swinging on a chain in front of him while praying for Fraco.

"What kind of a funeral is this? Whose idea was this? Was it my idiot son?"

Fie exchanged a glance with Sid when the shrill sound of Davet's mother's voice broke the reverent silence that had fallen over everyone along the peaceful hike. "You two keep going with Father Sterling. I'll deal with the trash."

Since their arrival, Davet's parents had gone out of their way to be a nuisance. They'd criticised every aspect of the day. His mother, in particular, had picked at her son ruthlessly.

"Uncle Santos said I couldn't disinvite them." Davet toyed with the ear of the fox.

"I'm not Santos." Fie left Sid and Davet to continue on the path.

In truth, Fie had been disappointed greatly by Davet's uncle. He'd known Santos Crisp-Ruiz for years. He'd always thought the man had more courage, along with care for his nephew.

How the hell isn't he telling his sister off for turning her son's memorial into a circus?

Waiting for the procession to pass by, Fie was surprised when Davet caught up to him. They stepped into the path to block his parents from continuing on. Fie stayed next to him to offer support.

Despite the obvious strain, Davet clearly wanted to be the one confronting his parents. He appeared quite close to the edge of his ability to process; a state Fie had experience with, though obviously with a different cause.

"Why are you here? Why turn this into a spectacle for yourselves? Couldn't you find the decency to behave just once?" Davet asked loudly. Fie didn't need to glance behind them to know the others had stopped walking to listen into the confrontation. "Today of all days. Fraco is dead. Let him rest in peace. It's not about you."

"You—"

"No." Davet cut his mother off sharply. "Can't you allow Fraco peace even in death?"

"Right." Sid slipped up next to Fie, stepping into the conversation when Davet and his father started cursing each other in French. "You lot keep going. This isn't an accident to watch like vultures. I'll take the rubbish back to the car park. Perhaps I'll have them escorted to the nearest train station to go back to France. They've overstayed their welcome."

"Show's over," Fie snapped at the avid watchers.

"Father Sterling?"

The priest managed to corral their rapt audience back on the walk. Fie waited for the group to continue on the path before turning towards the trembling Davet. Haggard sat beside the autistic, leaning against his leg to offer comfort.

"Shall we?" Fie asked when Davet had stopped muttering to himself in French. "Fraco would've loved this weather."

Weather?

Honestly?

Can I not do better than to suggest his dead brother would've loved the damned weather?

For God's sake.

"Fraco loved this walking path." Davet petted Haggard once and began to move forward. "I can do this."

They continued on in mostly silence, enjoying the sounds of the woods and the sea in the distance. Davet clutched the cuddly toy to his chest, repeating a phrase under his breath that Fie didn't quite make out. Sid caught up to them when they reached the shoreline.

Father Sterling waited until they'd all gathered around him. He glanced first at Davet, who kept staring at the waves. Fie caught the priest's eye and motioned for him to get started.

Yea, though I walk through the valley of the shadow of death. Surely goodness and mercy shall follow me all the days of my life: and I will dwell in the house of the Lord forever. Psalm 23: 4, 6

Once Father Sterling finished his liturgy, he quietly led the mourners away from the beach. Davet remained after a visibly reluctant hug with his aunt and uncle; he'd also handed the fox toy to his aunt for safekeeping. Fie and Sid both decided to remain, standing together to wait for the grieving young man.

Father Sterling had handed over the wooden chest with Fraco's ashes to Davet after praying one last time. They'd scattered some of the ashes along the path. Davet had walked to the edge of the water to slowly release his brother into the sea.

Fie stood shoulder to shoulder with Sid, enjoying the calm of the sea and not having a crowd around them. Haggard raced along the shoreline, darting after a stray bird before returning to check on all three of his charges. Fie had no doubts his furry friend considered anyone around him to be under his care.

"Do you believe in God?" Davet closed the lid on the carved wooden box, turning around to face them. "Is there really some greater purpose to all of this pain and suffering?"

"Maybe." Sid shrugged. "I've no idea. Swayze and I aren't really the altar boy types."

They lapsed into silence again. Fie didn't want to rush him. He was just thankful Davet's parents hadn't found a way to ruin the remainder of Fraco's memorial.

"I don't." Davet kicked a stray shell, sending it into the sea. "Can't after this."

"Understandable." Sid caught Davet when he stumbled, trying to kick at the sand again. "Easy there."

Davet shifted his gaze from Sid to Fie and back again. "Thank you for being here. For me. Both of you."

Before Fie could respond, he watched as Davet launched forward to grab Sid by the front of his coat and crush their lips together. *Fuck. Don't get turned on at the end of a funeral.* Fie didn't get a chance to think anything else, because Davet grabbed his jacket and snogged him as well.

"Merde." Davet grinned, covered his mouth, and raced off, muttering to himself in French.

Fie gaped at the fleeing Davet. Sid appeared equally stunned. *Right.* "Watson might've had a point. Time for us to have a chat about relationships, isn't it?"

"I vote for more snogging."

Fie pinched the bridge of his nose and counted to ten, then twenty just to be safe. "Chatting might involve our mouths, but that doesn't require our lips being connected."

"More fun if they are." Sid chuckled and dodged out of the way of Fie's kick. "Fine. We'll chat first without snogging."

"Magnanimous of you."

"Have you been reading the word of the month calendar again?"

CHAPTER EIGHTEEN

Davet

Six months had flown by for everyone—everyone but Davet. He'd struggled to maintain his life in Bideford. Without loyal customers who cared about him, his coffee shop would likely have closed doors.

The first few months had been the worst; Davet usually enjoyed the seasons changing from winter into spring. He'd hated February, especially, with love and hearts everywhere. Last year, when the world had been a brighter place, he'd made specially flavoured coffee with heart-shaped foam.

Not this year.

He'd kept the shop closed, just to avoid all the questions.

By the time spring melted into summer, Davet had begun to find breathing easier. Tears no longer kept him company every night before bed. He slowly returned to himself, even with the gaping hole in his heart.

Fox and Rabbit initially made healing harder. They reminded him of Fraco whenever Davet saw them frolicking together. He briefly considered rehoming them, but as the heaviness in his heart eased, their furry presence helped more than it hurt.

In the heat of summer, Davet often closed up shop early and went wandering along the paths surrounding Bideford. He'd find a field to sit alone for hours. The wind off the sea kept him company along with his thoughts.

Far too frequently, Davet found his mind turning to two familiar faces. He'd avoided Fie and Sid after the impetuous kiss on the beach. They'd taken his actions as a hint to never mention the moment ever, or so he assumed.

Why else have they chosen to pretend the kiss didn't happen?

Do they think I was overcome with grief?

What if they assumed my sadness made me do something out of character?

Merde.

His uncle Santos had proven a perfect example of grief making people do the strangest things. Davet had been puzzled by his uncle until his auntie had explained he felt an overwhelming sense of guilt at not intervening in his nephews' childhood.

As a result, Davet hadn't seen his uncle in months—tricky to do when they lived within a stone's throw of each other. He took his auntie's advice to wait him out.

She insisted the responsibility belonged to them, not either of her nephews. They had been innocent children in need of adults to step up and protect them.

"Adults failed. Not you," she'd insisted. "You let my Santos face his mistakes. He's strong enough to manage the emotional work. If not, I'll take my pan to his head."

So Davet had focused on himself for the first time in his life.

Even as a child, Davet's energy had gone mostly to protecting and helping Fraco, more parent than brother. After the sharp pain of grief dulled, he found an odd emptiness and restlessness. He had to discover a purpose beyond ensuring his brother's life went to plan.

"Isn't it farmers who hide out in their fields? Are you planning on changing careers?" Shirley often came out to join him with a novel and a packed lunch. "Four days in a row now I've had to trek into the wilds."

"It's hardly the wilds." Davet shrugged. He dodged the edge of the blanket when she flicked it out to place on the ground.

"Want some tea?" She set her basket on the blanket and sat down beside it. "I've got an hour and a half, a four cheese-and-bacon quiche, and an unfinished novel."

Davet lifted his copy of the book, which they'd been reading together as part of their book club for two. "Have you reached chapter twenty-seven yet?"

"Oh. My. God. I hate the author. Hate them." She quickly poured tea into cups, handing one over to him. "Stayed up half the night reading and fell asleep with my face in my Shreddies."

"You don't eat cereal." Davet stretched his legs out in front of him, batting away a stray fly. "You weren't serious."

"Not quite." Shirley offered a plate with half of the quiche and a few biscuits. "Never mind."

"I forgot." Davet shifted his legs up and rested the plate on his knee. "I forgot."

"What?" Shirley asked before taking a bite of her late lunch.

"It's hard to remember your normal conversation isn't the same as how it hits my brain." Davet had always worked so hard not to stand out; years of being humiliated by his parents had pounded it into him. He'd never managed to perfect masking. "Not sure why I bother trying to pretend. It's so much effort."

"Neither do I."

"You don't understand how painful standing out can be." Davet forced himself to eat despite his failing appetite.

"I probably don't." She reached out to tug lightly on his long-sleeved T-shirt. "I'm a black lesbian living in a small village in Devon. I might not know what being autistic is like, but I know all about not fitting into societal expectations and standing out. The stress of forcing yourself into their box can kill you."

She had a point.

On his annual visit, his doctor had encouraged him to lower his stress. *Drink less coffee, reduce the stressors in your life, and keep your blood pressure down.* Davet had refused to even consider medication. He'd promised to consider reducing his caffeine levels.

He'd been left with quite a dilemma. *How do I reduce stress in an allistic world that causes me anxiety just by being what it is?* He'd made the decision to try to be himself more and stop trying to push himself into the mould of a non-autistic.

But some days, it was incredibly hard.

And other days, completely impossible.

"Davet?"

He glanced up to find Shirley holding a cup of tea out to him. "I'm all right."

"Right." She eyed him for a moment then changed the subject with a grin. "Have you heard from your delicious duo?"

"No." Davet gulped down tea to clear the quiche from his mouth. "Well, yes, but not about the kiss. They come by for coffee and act painfully polite."

"Cowards."

"What if they aren't interested?" Davet didn't believe two war heroes were actually cowardly at all.

"Not a chance." Shirley had encouraged him to make a move for ages. "Why haven't you talked to them?"

"I can't." Davet set the cup down and fell back on

the blanket with a grown. "I'm not into humiliation. And I *am* a coward."

"You aren't. Have you considered they might be afraid they're taking advantage of you while you're in a delicate emotional state?" Shirley pointed her fork at him. "They're good blokes. They're probably waiting to be sure the kiss wasn't just you expressing your grief in a horny manner."

"In a horny manner?" Davet threw a stray wildflower at her. "It wasn't my grief talking."

"No, it was your cock. Men do that." She grabbed his arm to tug him up into a seated position. "Why haven't you told them? What if they decide to find another cub?"

"Oh my God. You need to stop reading romance novels." He covered his ears, glaring at her. "I'm not a cub."

Shirley had made a game out of attempting to numb him to innuendo. It never worked. She continued to tease him endlessly anyway.

"What? They're definitely bears."

"Shirley." Davet moved his hands from his ears to cover his face. "Why do you torment me?"

"Am I wrong? They're big, burly, bearded."

"If I promise to talk to Sid and Fie, will you stop?" he pleaded.

"Sure."

"Thank you."

"Mostly," Shirley added before holding out a slice

of cake.

"Merde." Davet begrudgingly took the plate from her. "You're insufferable."

They nattered about their book while finishing the cake and tea. When they'd wrapped up their book club meeting, Shirley badgered him into heading over to Fie's workshop. Her argument of "what can possibly go wrong?" didn't fill him with an excess of confidence.

Off the top of his head, Davet had already thought of six ways the conversation might end badly. He walked home to check on Fox and Rabbit. The latter went with him on the trek from his cottage to Fie's place.

The short walk took him thirty minutes. Davet kept finding distractions, places to wander off the path. He almost turned around to go home twice but continued on as Shirley would probably text him in the evening to ask how it went and harass him all over again if she found out he'd chickened out.

Right. What is the worst thing they can possibly do? Turn me down? How's that any different from my position now?

Go say hello.

Say more than hello, or we'll still be in the same position.

CHAPTER NINETEEN

S<small>ID</small>

"Sid?" Jacinda slid into his office on her wheeled chair, bumping into his desk and almost falling over. "Where's your final report on the Heuse death? Did you find any legitimate reason to keep the case open or pursue his roommates for furthering questioning?"

Sid shifted through the stacks of paper on his desk to find the one he'd been putting off. "Here."

Despite his gut feeling on Fraco's death and his best efforts, Sid hadn't been able to make any progress. Pressure had built for him to officially close his investigation. He'd put it off for as long as possible.

"You did your job." Jacinda grabbed the report from him, patted his arm with it, and wheeled herself out of his office. "There's chocolate cake in the break room. Theo brought leftovers from his sprog's birthday. I made sure to save you a piece before the vultures descended."

"Did you lick it?"

"Me? I would never." Jacinda's grin told him everything he needed to know. "Maybe a little. It's chocolate on chocolate on chocolate. How could I resist?"

"Just have the cake." Sid tapped his fingers against his desk. "I should tell Davet the case is closed."

"You should. In person." She pushed herself off the wall with her foot to continue gliding over to her own office. "I'm eating the cake."

"Course you are." Sid dug around on his desk to find his keys and mobile. He didn't want to delay giving Davet the bad news.

Despite his best intentions, Sid found himself driving toward Fie's and avoiding Davet's cottage and coffee shop altogether. *I am a massive cowardly giant. And apparently fond of redundant statements. Fuck me.*

"MacFluff." Fie didn't even bother standing up to greet him when Sid walked into his workshop. He stayed bent over a mug. "I'm busy."

Ignoring the curt dismissal, Sid wandered over to pet the sleeping Haggard and then perched on a nearby stool. He eyed Fie for a minute to gauge his mood. It paid to keep track of how Fie was feeling before chatting with him.

Sid took Haggard's relaxed position as a green light. "I had to close the investigation into Fraco's death."

"Damn." Fie set the mug down and twisted around on his seat. "No chance of finding answers?"

"Not in my official capacity." Sid didn't fancy risking his career to push on with questioning when all evidence pointed towards an accidental drowning. "How do I tell Davet?"

"No." Fie held his hand up immediately. "I'm not doing the dirty work for you. Tell him yourself."

"He's not talking to either of us at the moment. Not beyond a hello." Sid didn't know if it was them not talking to Davet or the reverse, but their usually comfortable chats had devolved into awkwardness ever since Fraco's funeral. "Did we bugger up our chance by not addressing the kiss at the time?"

"Probably." Fie scratched at his beard absently. "Maybe don't bring kissing up when you disappoint him regarding the investigation, yeah?"

"And here I thought you might be helpful." He tossed a clump of clay at Fie's head. "Wanker."

"Me?" Fie caught the clay, setting it aside carefully while glaring at Sid. "Watch it, MacFluff."

"Why would he fancy either of us? Let alone being attracted to both of us at the same time." Sid voiced the question he knew had plagued Fie as well. "Kissing aside."

"We're not hideous."

"I'd fancy us." Sid held a hand up to stop Fie from responding. "I know, you already do."

A quiet snicker drew their attention to the doorway where Davet stood with a fox dancing around his feet.

Sid groaned.

Right.

Well, I've only managed to make this even more awkward. I'm a sodding genius. Fuck.

They all stared at each other.

Well, not entirely. Davet's gaze appeared to hover somewhere in the space between Sid and Fie.

We're all absolutely hopeless at this.

"Would you both feel less awkward if we got the first fuck out of the way?" Sid asked with a wicked smile. "We can agonise over who asks who out afterwards. Shag now, converse later." He paused when they both frowned at him. "Shall I take your silent glares as a no?"

"Sid." Fie rubbed his hand across his face with a muffled groan. "How is that making any of this less awkward?"

Sid couldn't help his slightly hysterical bark of laughter. "Can't make it worse, can it?"

"Yes, yes it can." Fie pointed toward Davet, who seemed unsure of whether to bolt out the door or remain to watch the spectacular train wreck happening in front of him. "Do you try to be difficult?"

"Gifted."

Davet inched further into the room. "Hello."

"I invited you to shag. Think we're beyond hello." Sid grunted when Fie whacked him in the stomach. "What? Am I wrong?"

"I kissed you," Davet uttered into the silence. "Both."

"True." Sid didn't need the second nudge from Fie to wait out the clearly uncomfortable Davet. "We didn't mind."

Davet became intensely interested in his fox. Rabbit darted around the room until deciding to curl up on top of Haggard, who didn't even open his eyes. "I kissed you."

"Yes." Fie nodded.

"I kissed you." Davet echoed himself several more times. Sid had researched enough how being autistic affected a person to know repetition could be part and parcel of it. "And you never said anything—either of you. Was I terrible?"

"Did you miss the invitation to sha—" Sid grunted for a second time when Fie nudged him hard enough to cause him to fall off the chair. "Will you stop that?"

"When you stop throwing around invitations to shag. We're not at the fucking point yet." Fie stood up and went to check on the kiln. "Have you eaten yet? Either of you?"

"Are you going to play mother?" Sid teased.

Finishing up at the kiln, Fie clearly decided to ignore the playful dig. He invited Davet and Sid into his cottage for tea and snacks. The latter turned out to be a variety of biscuits and savoury cheddar and bacon scones his mum had sent.

Fie did *not* play mother. Sid did. He made better tea, and keeping occupied made him less likely to open his mouth and ruin their chances with Davet, who perched on the edge of a chair in the kitchen as if preparing to make a run for it at the first chance if necessary.

They all needed to calm down.

"We've kissed, barely a chaste peck on the lips." Sid decided to address the situation head-on. "Fie and I didn't mind. Fair to say we'd have enjoyed a less innocent version even more. We didn't chat with you about it afterwards because you were grieving. And what kind of pricks would we be to take advantage of you at that moment?"

We'd have been massive giant pricks.

Despite Fie being the more sensitive (and grumpy) of the two friends, Sid had agreed wholeheartedly with waiting for Davet to approach them. Or, he had initially. His confidence had wavered when a few weeks turned into months and almost half a year had gone by since those surprising but not unwelcome kisses.

"And you wouldn't mind kissing?" Davet clutched a handful of biscuits tightly, crumbs falling to the floor unnoticed by him—but not the dog and fox. "Again."

"Why don't we go out for dinner?" Fie suggested, much to Sid's surprise. He usually avoided crowded restaurants, even with Haggard beside him.

Granted, Davet likely dealt with a similar issue though for different reasons than Fie's post-traumatic stress. Sid wracked his brain for a solution. He wanted their first attempt at a date to go as smoothly as possible.

"Battered."

Fie paused in the middle of biting into a biscuit.

"Battered. Brilliant, MacFluff."

Battered was owned by an older couple who'd lived in Bideford for ages. They only opened on the weekends now. Sid quickly got on his phone to see if they'd open up for the evening as a favour to their favourite police detective.

After a bit of sweet talking, Sid managed to get the restaurant to themselves for a quiet Friday supper. His elation at succeeding faded quickly when he remembered why he'd wanted to speak with Davet in the first place. *For fuck's sake. This isn't exactly going to put him in the mood, is it?*

Pull your bootstraps up and get on with it.

"You've gone quiet." Davet crumbled one of the biscuits in his fingers, obviously sensing some of the stress in the room. "Was it the kissing?"

"No." Sid smothered his urge to laugh; he thought Davet might misunderstand his reaction. "Definitely nothing to do with the kissing. I planned on driving over to see you later to talk about my investigation."

"Oh." Davet visibly deflated in front of them, sinking into his chair. He dumped the biscuit pieces onto a napkin and brought his legs up to rest his feet on the edge of the seat with his arms wrapped around them. "You didn't find anything, did you?"

"You must be psychic." Sid chuckled awkwardly.

"Why else would you be so uneasy about telling me?" Davet's shoulders dropped. "You're uncomfortable. You didn't want to speak to me about Fraco. I'd guess the investigation didn't go anywhere."

Sid grabbed one of the other chairs, shifting over to sit in front of Davet. "There is no evidence to even hint at Fraco's death being anything other than a tragic accident."

Aside from my instincts telling me that his little shit roommates had a part to play.

"Fine." Davet didn't sound like he meant the word. He dropped his feet to the floor and slowly sat up straight. "Nothing to do now but move on."

Haggard got up, dislodging Rabbit the not-bunny, and headed over. He sat in front of Davet and rested his head on his knee. Sid always marvelled at how well the dog sensed the mood of those around him.

Sid thought they'd need more than Haggard and the not-bunny to cheer Davet up. "Why don't we go out for ice cream?"

"Because we're not ten?" Fie glowered over his cup.

"So? It's summer and bloody hot. Let's go for ice cream." Sid had learned from dealing with Fie that allowing someone to brood often made it harder to move beyond whatever had caused the depression. "Sun is out. We can even walk down the beach."

"Pennecombe?"

"If you like." Sid wasn't sure if revisiting Fraco's favourite beach would help or hurt Davet. "Ready?"

"Does this count as a date?" Davet asked after they'd made their way outside.

"Only if kissing is involved." Sid wiggled his eyebrows, hoping to inject a small amount of levity after a difficult conversation. "Snogging definitely adds to the date-like nature of the excursion."

"Macfluff!"

CHAPTER TWENTY

F IE

Three grown men eating ice cream on the beach. What are we doing? This feels far more bizarre than it actually is.

Fie tried to turn off his inner dialogue without much success.

"We're like the beginning of a bad porno." Sid gave his ice cream a long lick. "Are you turned on?"

"Have I ever mentioned what a massive wanker you are?" Fie turned away from Sid to keep from laughing, grateful Davet wasn't in hearing range. *He's not wrong, though.* "Not on a first date, MacFluff."

They'd found a Hocking's van to grab double-scoop cones. Sid had immediately stolen Fie's Flake. *Wanker.* Davet had practically inhaled his chocolate to avoid the same fate.

Their ice cream barely lasted down to the beach. Fie felt like a kid again with vanilla stickiness dripping down his fingers. *Shit. We are like a bad porno.* He had to admit, at least to himself, that his mood had lifted considerably.

"Can I lick your fingers?" Sid teased.

"No." Fie stared down at the remnants of his ice cream cone, then smashed the lot into Sid's face. "Lick that."

"Do you always play with your food?" Davet had returned from his stroll along the shoreline. He'd gotten emotional when they arrived; Fie had sent Haggard off to keep him company. "How will this work?"

Fie motioned with his hand, and Haggard leapt on Sid, who fell backwards. "Oi!" Haggard licked at Sid's face to get at the ice cream. "Call your attack dog off, Swayze."

Fie whistled for Haggard, who moved over and flopped on his side next to his human with his tongue lolling out. "You changed your mind about getting your face licked quickly."

For a brief moment, Fie was reminded of the days before Afghanistan, the years when he'd been as prone to mucking about and laughing as Sid. He often struggled to remember that man. His friends worried about him because he'd returned so different.

Sullen.

Fie wondered if whatever this turned into might bring him back to himself a little more. He glanced toward Davet, who just seemed confused. "How will what work?"

"This." He gestured vaguely at the three of them. "Won't people find us dating odd?"

"Three men? Or two older men perving on a younger one?" Sid queried with a laugh. "Do we really care what stuffed-up numpties think?"

For the hundredth time, Fie wondered how anyone had believed his old friend capable of being a serious police detective. Davet had a point, though. Small villages occasionally translated to close-mindedness.

Maybe they'd be proven wrong.

"We've barely gotten through the first date. Why don't we hold off on making action plans to deal with homophobic pricks until we manage more than a kiss on the lips and an ice cream together?" Fie rubbed absently at his beard, smiling at how innocent their interactions sounded. "Have we gone back in time to the fifties?"

"No, because we haven't been arrested and medically castrated for being gay." Sid pulled a napkin out of his pocket and wiped at his face. "So, we won't be time travelling to when society was a bunch of homophobic wankers, will we?"

"I am confused." Davet knelt in the sand with his fox balanced on his shoulder. "Are we dating or…. I don't understand."

What are we doing? Fie couldn't help agreeing with the bewildered tone in Davet's voice.

Polyamory was outside of the scope of Fie's usual relationships. *Not that I've had many in the last few years.* Shagging Sid didn't count, particularly as they'd gone out of their way not to discuss it afterwards. He hoped whatever they were doing became more than one night in bed.

Stop thinking about Sid and Davet naked on the sand.

You're old enough to have some self-control.

"We're having ice cream. And Friday, we're going to eat food—probably pie of some sort." Sid broke the silence that had fallen. "We're going to get to know one another better as more than friends. Defining it before it's started is asking for trouble."

"I like defining things." Davet drew designs in the sand at his feet. "Less chance for misunderstanding."

"We're eating ice cream and contemplating a bit of wanking," Sid offered.

"I'm contemplating a wanker." Fie thought Sid's attempt to alleviate some of Davet's stress might be backfiring. "Let's take it a step at a time. First one? Ice cream, dinner, and Sid playing with himself."

General confusion and silliness aside, Fie wondered how many relationships Davet had experienced. He might need more a more in-depth conversation if he'd never dealt with a romantic or sexual entanglement—or both. *Is Sid capable of being a pleasant first time for someone?*

Fuck.

Fie caught Sid's attention with a tap of his forefinger to his ear, a signal from their military days to quieten him down. He returned his attention to Davet in the hopes of sussing out more information. *Delicately. Us? Subtle probing? We're buggered right up, and not in a fun way.*

"Sid and I are both old enough to have quite a history between us of…." Oddly flustered by the topic, Fie trailed off mid-sentence. *Is it patronising to ask about this? We have to know. Don't we?*

Am I making a massive deal about something small?

"Are you going to finish your question?" Davet crossed his legs and leaned forward with his elbows on his knees. "You seem uneasy. Can never tell. Is it uneasy? Or angry?"

"Uneasy," Fie clarified for him. He'd noticed Davet struggled to sort out emotions and tone. "Have you dated much?"

"No." Davet's gaze shifted from the sand to Fie's nose. He went quiet for a few seconds. "I'm not a virgin."

Well.

"All right."

"Are you?" Davet rolled his eyes with a dramatic sigh. "Does it matter? You'll be as confusing to me whether I've had a hundred partners or none. You're not asking Sid."

"Fair enough." Sid shrugged.

"I don't want to have any misunderstandings or take advantage." Fie had always believed in having everything out on the table.

Davet narrowed his eyes on them; well, more their

noses than anything. "Why are you so focused on if I've had sex? Actually, I've always wanted to know why allistics say you've lost your virginity. I didn't forget where I put it. Jacques, when I was sixteen, in his parents' car, which was uncomfortable and messy. And Simone at eighteen. She managed better. Still awkward. I know where I left my virginities. I'm bisexual, not suffering from memory loss."

"Right." Sid smirked at Fie. "I think he'll be fine, you old worrywart."

"I don't believe in jumping in feet first without making sure everyone's on the same page." Fie knew with him still fighting his way out of the mire of post-traumatic stress and Davet being autistic, they'd all manage better if they over-communicated rather than assuming. "Don't be an arse."

"How about jumping in cock first?"

"Sounds painful." Davet shuddered.

"Sand is sticking to my face." Sid hadn't been entirely successful in wiping off the ice cream. "Anyone have water?"

"There's the sea." Davet pointed to it. "Have a swim."

"He's got jokes."

"Says the man who suggested jumping in cock first." Fie shoved Sid back on the sand.

CHAPTER TWENTY-ONE

Davet

Allistics, Davet had found, tended to overcomplicate their lives, particularly when it came to sex and sexuality. He'd also noticed they unintentionally seemed to believe him incapable of adult behaviour as though being autistic meant remaining childlike forever.

Have I ever been in a relationship? Am I a virgin? Merde.

I'm in my twenties, definitely not asexual or aromantic. Yes, I've explored my sexuality.

Ça me fait chier.

What was the word Sid used?

Wankers.

Sex had been the easiest aspect of exploring relations. Romance bewildered him, as did the expectations that came with it. His lovers had seemed to instinctually know the rules, and he'd missed the day the rulebook was handed out.

In some ways, Davet appreciated Fie's insistence on talking the subject to death. Better to be 100 percent clear than screw it up later because someone didn't understand, and the scales were definitely weighted toward him being the one to get the wrong end. The conversation had brought up memories from being home in France.

Jacques had been his first interlude with another man. Davet had learnt several important lessons, mostly how much he hated all the moistness involved. Condoms had become a must for him just to avoid the sensations that could trigger a meltdown for him.

Meltdowns in the middle of sex tended to ruin the happy buzz.

He shuddered just at the thought of it.

Moist and sticky.

It set his entire body on edge to even think about. Davet wondered if Sid and Fie would be put off by his quirk. He couldn't help how his brain chose to interpret sensations.

His other first, Simone, had left an equally important impression on him. She'd encouraged him to fight for his and Fraco's freedom. Davet had also learnt from her to be proud of his bisexual nature.

Never believe anyone who insists you have to love one over the other.

As they grew into adulthood, Jacques had left for America to study. Simone had pursued her education in Paris. They both kept in touch via email. He'd poured his heart out to Simone several times recently over his attraction to both Sid and Fie.

Her response had been quintessential Simone. She'd told him to enjoy both and send pictures for her to live vicariously through him. Davet appreciated the support but didn't quite feel the need to quench her voyeuristic thirst; plus, Sid and Fie wouldn't likely approve.

A day after her message, Davet realised she'd been joking. Probably. Simone had a devilish sense of humour. He hated having to ask if she were serious, so he made an educated guess and just ignored that part of her email.

The encouragement had helped him gear up for dinner. His nerves threatened to derail everything, as did his overthinking. He didn't know if he'd even be able to eat with his stomach doing the tango.

Dress nicely, be yourself, slip under the table to suck them off.

Simone had offered the first two while Jacques had been his usual self with the last piece of advice. He ignored the latter for the moment. They might wind up chased out of the village with pitchforks.

And Davet had no idea if whether dress nicely meant comfortably or fancy. *Does be myself involve acting normally according to society, or skipping the masking and being my glorious autistic myself? Merde. I am so nervous.*

He'd agreed to meet Sid and Fie at Battered.

Walking to the restaurant would hopefully ease some of the stress. *Or give me far too much time to think about all the ways the date will go horribly wrong.*

An hour later, Davet had his entire wardrobe spread across his bed, chair, and floor. Rabbit and Fox had curled up together after inspecting the clothes and getting fur on everything. *Right, be myself—with fur.*

Sitting on the edge of the bed, Davet buried his face in his hand. Could he do this? Was it wrong to be happy again after six months?

Since Fraco's death, Davet had struggled with a dark depression. The short winter days had compounded the issue; life had seemed all doom and gloom to him. Therapy had helped.

Jane had recommended a friend who lived in the area. They apparently supplied service animals to some of his clients. Davet struggled to go into the office so much the therapist had made a house call instead.

It helped.

Slowly.

The grief no longer threatened to drown him underneath the weight of how much he missed his brother. Weekends were the hardest. Davet often watched the door, expecting Fraco to rush in with his latest rescued creature.

Okay, breathe in and out, Davet.

Let's focus on clothes and not devolve into tears before my first dinner date in ages.

Do I go for the black shirt with fox fur or the

burgundy with strands of rabbit? Jeans with both?

I can do this.

Making the journey to Battered didn't actually lower his stress at all. Davet arrived thirty minutes early. He sat on a bench outside reciting his favourite Yves Bonnefoy poem to himself. One he'd memorised in both French and the English translation, "They spoke to Me."

The poem had comforted him during tumultuous times with his parents. Words, Davet had found, healed as much as they hurt. He allowed the poem to wash over him and his heart rate slowly returned to normal.

"Want to come in, lad?"

The Evanses invited him inside after obviously spotting his pathetic form outside. Davet found a flush of embarrassment had replaced his stress. *Who arrives half an hour before a date?*

Me, because I'm pathetic.

"Aren't you sweet? All nervous for your date." Mrs. Evans patted his cheek and turned toward the kitchen. "Settle yourself down, love, while I get back to work."

"We've set you over here by the window at the back. Great view of our garden without anyone peeking in on you. Have a seat." Mr. Evans guided him over to the cosy table. "We made our veggie pie and the steak and ale one, plus a fancy surprise for pudding."

"Thank you." Davet shifted uneasily, worried about their reaction to a relationship between three men. With any luck, the Evanses openness would be the norm and not the exception. He wasn't holding his breath, having experienced all sorts of bigotry over the years. "Sorry I'm so early. Hope I haven't thrown you off."

Mr Evans waved away Davet's apology. "Never you mind. I showed up early for my first night with my darling Sarah. She made me wait anyway."

Left to himself, Davet fidgeted in his seat. He wanted to go home, change into more comfortable clothes, and binge watch *Spooks*. The show about MI-6 was one of his favourites, which he tended to watch on repeat on bad days.

Or on days when being social is beyond me.
What if they don't show up?

Being alone in a restaurant with no other customers only highlighted how early he'd arrived. Davet went from the seat to stand by the window, then back to sit down. *Why did I give myself all this extra time to panic?*

Sid and Fie arrived within moments of each other. Davet picked at the stray fur on his trousers, getting up to meet them. He waved, unsure of the greeting etiquette for a second date with two men.

Shake hands?
No.
A kiss? Not before dinner, and not with an audience.
Do something, it's getting awkward.
What would Simone do? All right, not doing that.
"Hello." Davet waved again.
Oh, yes, you've impressed them.

"Been here long?" Sid asked. He dragged Davet into a hug.

Davet decided not to think about how good Sid smelled. "Not too long."

"Showed up early, he did." Mr Evans ratted him out, coming out of the kitchen with two pints of beer and a glass of water. "Now, sit yourselves down. We'll have a bit of a nibble out for you soon."

"I wasn't that early." Davet hoped he'd hit the bottom of the humiliation bucket for the evening. "Only slightly."

Silence.

They sat in awkward silence, staring at their drinks. Davet wondered if maybe they should already call it a night and try again. He knew a date required small talk—he just didn't know how to start.

"We managed on the beach with ice cream." Sid broke the quiet after a long swig of beer. "How hard can this dinner be?"

"Not very. We're not cooking." Fie grabbed one of the breadsticks on the table. "We just have to pretend we know how to converse with each other on a proper date."

"Fairly confident most of the country will consider it improper for three blokes to be on a date in the first place." Sid took one of the breadsticks and pushed the plate toward Davet. "Eat. We'll relax. Are we date virgins?"

"Triple date virgins."

Davet stared at both of them. "For men with such experience, you're obsessed with the idea of virginity. Was yours traumatic? People usually get stuck on subjects when they had a difficult time."

Sid laughed loudly, spewing crumbs everywhere. "Were you traumatised, Swayze?"

"I am not having this conversation with Mr and Mrs Evans, who are old enough to be my nan and granddad, eavesdropping." Fie pointed his breadstick at Sid. "Why don't we all take a deep breath? Hmm? In and out. Settle ourselves down. It's only dinner with elderly peeping toms, nothing to cause undue tension."

"Aside from me wanting to shag you both over the table?" Sid asked.

"Aside from that, yes." Fie's lips twitched as though he wanted to laugh. "Can we all attempt to behave ourselves? You're a sodding police detective. We'll give our hosts a bad impression."

The two men bantered back and forth while Davet watched them. He used their conversation to take time to settle his mind. Their ease with each other actually went a great way toward helping him relax.

Nibbles turned out to be miniature Yorkshire puddings with a variety of savoury fillings. Davet fought Sid for the sausage and mash ones. Fie appeared content to allow them to argue over them while he secretly ate the majority of the rest.

"You sneaky wanker." Sid glared at the now empty platter. "I didn't even get to try the reddish one."

With the appetisers eaten, Mr Evans brought out beautifully browned pies for them. Davet's mouth watered just from the smell alone. He didn't know how the date was going, but the food part had been beautiful thus far.

They never made it to the special pudding or flirting with an after dinner kiss. Sid received a text on his work mobile and stormed out, muttering something about his father. Davet was left staring in confusion at Fie.

"His father didn't handle the news of his personal preferences well."

"About?" Davet didn't quite understand Fie's point. "His job?"

"His sexual preferences."

"Oh." Davet glanced at the front door of the restaurant. "Should we follow?"

"No, but let's go anyway." Fie got to his feet with a groan.

CHAPTER TWENTY-TWO

S<small>ID</small>

Jacinda: Your old man is here looking for you. Didn't think you'd want him intruding on the date, but he's getting rather red in the face over my delaying him.

The date, his dinner, and his rather imaginative sexual fantasies flew out of his mind in a second. Sid's entire focus turned to getting back to the police station before his dad managed to completely damage his reputation. People often had trouble remembering "like father, like son" wasn't always warranted.

I'm not a bigoted dipshit.

And he definitely is.

After jogging to his vehicle and driving to the station, Sid arrived to find a less than patient Jacinda glaring holes in his dad's head. He was as oblivious as always. His father appeared to be in the middle of a one-sided conversation about how he'd come around to his son's bad choices in life.

Can I sneak away before either of them spots me?
Probably, but Jacinda would murder me in my sleep.

"Sid." Jacinda had never seemed so relieved to see him. "Thank Christ. Deal with the man who made you."

"Listen, you—"

Sid grabbed his father by the arm and led him forcibly down the hall toward his office in the hopes of heading off what would be an impressive explosion if Jacinda went off like dynamite. And she'd have every right. "Why are you here?"

"You're my only son."

"I was your only son when you called me a name I won't repeat and told me to never speak to you again." Sid collapsed into his chair, gesturing more calmly than he felt to the seat across from him. "I buggered off at your request. Why are you here? Are you dying? Catch some disease? Or was it a course on how to actually be a father?"

"I am *not* diseased or dying. Well, not immediately. I'm getting older." His father went silent as if waiting for him to respond. He sighed with an irritated huff when Sid didn't. "I'm getting older, and you are my only son."

"Well spotted." Sid eased back in his chair, tilting back to stare up at the ceiling while counting to fifty. He regretted not having finished his supper, since undoubtedly all of his patience and strength would be required. "Why now? You were quite happy to write me off all this time. I haven't changed. Still enjoy cock, not kitty."

"I raised you better." His father slapped his hand against the desk.

"Are you complaining about my language, my orientation, or both?" Sid had gotten beyond his heartbreak at being tossed from the family. He refused to bend over backwards in an effort to worm his way back in. "I abandoned a hot date to rush over here. Did you have something new to say or should I escort you to your car?"

"I'm old."

"So you've said." Sid tried not to think about how his date night should've ended. It only served to frustrate him further. "We've both gotten older. Time does that to a person. I'm more interested in whether it's taught you to be less of a bigoted wanker."

"Show me some respect, boy."

"I'm not a boy, and I'll show you respect when you deserve it."

"Your mother would've hated how we fought." His father shifted uneasily. "She loved both of us."

"Mum knew I was gay." Sid had never come out to her, but they'd danced around the conversation once, and her response had left him with no doubt. "She loved me—no changes to who I am required."

"Not natural," he insisted stubbornly. "You're a man. A Little. Tall, muscled."

Sid scrubbed a tired hand across his face. He refused to repeat this painful conversation for the second time; the first one still haunted his dreams on occasion. "I served in the military. I am a detective inspector. None of that relates to my sexuality. It's all a part of who I am. No one turned me. I didn't catch some disease. I was born gay. Go home if you can't love me as I am."

"I'm lonely." His father admitted after a lengthy silence that involved them glaring at each other. "House is too quiet. No kids or grandchildren."

And whose fault is that then? Not mine.

"Well, you're out of luck on the sprogs issue. I'm not having any. I can barely keep my plant alive." He gestured toward his Christmas gift from Jacinda, which appeared to be dead. "Shit. Forgot to water the thing."

"I want you in my life."

"I didn't keep you out of my life." Sid refused to allow guilt to be heaped on his shoulders by his father when he'd been the one tossed out on his ear. "Can we not talk in circles? I'm tired. I've left pudding on the table, and I missed kissing two sexually attractive men."

"*Sidney.*"

"Yes?" Sid sat forward in his chair, resting his elbows on his desk. "Aren't you tired of being lonely?"

"Why do you think I'm here?"

"Not a sodding clue." Sid honestly had no idea what the point of his father travelling to Bideford was. They hadn't talked in ages, and his old man didn't appear to have anything new to say. And Sid had no intentions of locking himself into the closet to make him comfortable. "I'm not changing."

His father grumped loudly and shifted in his chair. "Your mother would've hoped we'd find a compromise."

A compromise.

Sid breathed out noisily and massaged his forehead. "How exactly do you see us finding middle ground?"

"Live and let live."

"Really?" Sid chuckled bitterly. His father had grimaced when he spoke, not exactly an encouraging sign. "It's late. You should head home. You might miss your favourite programme on the telly."

They stared at each other. Sid, in his heart, didn't want to slam the door in his father's face. He also refused to subject either Fie or Davet to any vitriol whether subtle or blatant.

Or myself.

I deserve better from my father.

Sid felt the tight band around his heart ease at the truth in those words. In their relationship, aside from harsh words, he'd done nothing wrong. "You taught me to be my own person. And I am."

"You aren't willing to try?"

He met his father's gaze without flinching. "Does trying involve me pretending to be straight in your presence?"

"Just don't parade it in front of me."

"Do you hear yourself?" Sid gripped the arms of his chair hard enough to cause the leather to groan. "If I'd married some random woman, I could fuck in the garden, and you'd be thrilled. Just so long as I wasn't with a man."

"I don't want to fight."

"Good. Neither do I." Sid forced himself to relax to avoid snapping the arms of his chair. "I won't compromise with you on this issue. I'm not pretending to be someone I'm not to appease your sensibilities. You're more concerned about me being gay than you were about the possibility of me dying in combat."

"I've obviously wasted my petrol." His father got to his feet, walking slowly toward the door as if expecting to be stopped at any moment. He paused to glance over his shoulder at Sid. "I worried every day you were at war."

"And you threw me away when you had me home safely because you misread your Bible." Sid refused to give an inch. "Drive safely. It's getting dark outside."

The silence deafened him. Sid collapsed against the seat as the tension drained out of his body. He felt exhausted and about a hundred years old all of a sudden.

"You all right?" Jacinda poked her head into his office. She stepped inside when he failed to answer. "So, I tried not to eavesdrop."

"Liar."

She set a chocolate bar on the desk in front of him.

"You might need this more than me."

"Are you telling me to eat my feelings?" Sid grabbed the chocolate before she could snatch it back. "I appreciate your sacrifice."

"Good, you owe me a replacement." Jacinda grinned when he rolled his eyes. "For what it's worth, you did the right thing. Your father should be proud of you."

"I'm not giving the chocolate back." He broke it in half and slid part toward her. "Thanks."

"Cheers." Jacinda slouched into the chair across from him. She snapped off a cube of the sweet and popped it into her mouth. "I like how you're repaying my kindness with my own chocolate."

"I'm a giver."

CHAPTER TWENTY-THREE

Fie

"Right." Fie and Davet stood on the pavement outside of the restaurant. He had their takeaway pudding clutched in a paper bag in one hand with Haggard attempting to sneak a sniff at his side. *How do I end a first date when Sid's disappeared on us? Can this get any more uncomfortable? Of course, it can.* "I'm going to check on MacFluff. Take him some cake."

"Together." Davet had his hands shoved into his pockets and his gaze focused off in the direction of the police station. "Walk?"

"Probably good to walk off all the food." Fie hated driving, particularly at night. He breathed through the sudden anxiety brought on by the idea of getting behind the wheel in the dark and the memories of another night when everything had gone wrong. Haggard bumped his nose into Fie's hand. "I'm all right."

He wasn't.

Exercise would help, and the sweat on his brow could easily be explained away by the balmy summer air. Davet strolled along beside him in silence. Fie appreciated the easy quiet.

"Is his father like my parents?" Davet asked when they were a few minutes away from the police building.

"Not quite." Fie considered the comparison. It wasn't entirely fair. Sid had known love from his father right up until he'd broken away from the man's vision of a perfect son. "Different situations, both painfully damaging to the soul, I imagine."

Imagining the rough relationships Sid and Davet suffered through with their families didn't come easy. Fie had always felt incredibly lucky with his family. They'd all supported and loved him, even when he pushed them away.

It was hard to justify ignoring his family when Fie saw the effects of unhealthy familial relationships around him. His mum's care packages meant the world to him. *I should probably tell her.*

"Will he be all right?" Davet rubbed his arm while he walked, having bumped into a post box, a car, and a gate.

"Will you? I've never seen someone literally bang their way down a pavement." Fie had been tempted to wrap his arm around Davet to keep him from playing bumper cars with his body. "How are you not just covered in bruises?"

Davet yanked up his shirtsleeve to point at one

behind his elbow. "No idea where this one came from. I found it yesterday. My spatial awareness isn't what yours is."

Fie grabbed him by the sleeve to keep him from heading into a shrub. "You worry me."

"I've never broken anything," Davet promised. "Not from running into a wall."

"Or the hedgerow?" Fie took the steps up two at the time. They found Jacinda chatting with a few other officers by the front doors. "Sid still here?"

Jacinda nodded toward a door down the hall that led deeper into the station. "Left him in the office pretending not to mope."

"Can we check on him?" Fie had been a few times but always asked in case someone took offence to a random bloke wandering through the station. "Maybe get him out of here."

"Go on, then." She grinned at him. "No naughtiness in his office. I've got to sit in there."

Ignoring the chuckling behind them, Fie made his way through the door that led to an open room with offices along the sides. Davet followed close behind. Fie had to sternly avoid chuckling when he managed to bump into a doorway, filing cabinet, and the wall.

They found Sid in his office with his head resting on his desk. A packet of crisps and a box of Jaffa Cakes rested beside him. He'd obviously raided someone else's desk for comfort food.

"Fancy a dark chocolate and strawberry swiss roll?"

Fie dangled the bag beside Sid's head. "How'd things go with Sidney the elder?"

"Oh, just fucking brilliant." Sid sat up and grabbed the bag before Fie could pull it away. "Hasn't changed a bit. Still expects me to spontaneously find tits attractive and populate the earth with my sprogs."

"The entire earth?" Davet asked curiously. He picked up one of the packets of crisps and peered inside. "Can one person do that?"

"Not without Viagra." Sid grabbed one of the slices of swiss roll, cramming it into his mouth. "He kept telling me he was old."

"He is." Fie took one of the spare seats across from Sid. "The older you get, the more all your mistakes haunt you. I imagine he's afraid of dying alone."

"Maybe he's afraid of dying without anyone to remember him." Davet had begun to fold the crisp packet into random shapes. "What is he leaving behind? What if the only memories you have of him are filled with pain? His legacy of being a good father and man will be gone forever. His fault, yes, but he doesn't know how to fix it."

Sid and Fie both stared in surprise. Davet continued playing with the packet. He didn't appear aware of their attention.

Every so often on their coffee mornings, Fie had been taken off-guard by the way Davet approached life. He had a unique perspective on things.

They chatted for a few minutes while fighting over

the last slice of cake. Davet won by simply reaching between them and shoving it into his mouth with a snicker at their outraged faces. Their playful argument drew Jacinda, who kicked them out of the station.

Sid stood on the top step outside. He seemed a little lost to Fie, who knew his old friend would probably spend the entire night thinking about the situation with his father if left to his own devices. "Now what?"

Their date had ended so abruptly. None of them seemed ready for the evening to be over, particularly with a less than cheerful mood. Sid could think of a number of activities to perk up the evening, but he refused to rush their relationship.

It's only a second date.

Patience is a virtue, and I'm not Sid.

"Home." Davet jogged down the steps. "Rabbit and Fox might eat each other."

"Five quid on the rabbit." Sid bent forward to whisper to Fie.

"Rabbit or the rabbit?" Fie asked. "How do you tell them apart?"

"One has floppy ears." Sid grinned.

Fie shoved him, then started forward to keep up with Davet. "One with the floppy ears, my arse."

Like two overgrown shadows, they followed Davet through Bideford to his little cottage. He opened the back door, and Rabbit immediately raced out to begin playing with Haggard. *Fox and the hound part two?* Fie couldn't help thinking Fraco would've loved to see it.

Davet wiped at his eyes roughly. He grabbed one of the spare milk crates, flipping it over and sitting to watch the fox and dog. "I miss Fraco. Sometimes it hurts so bad my lungs feel like they've frozen in my chest."

Fie exchanged a glance with Sid before they both grabbed crates of their own and sat on either side of Davet. "I'm so sorry."

"And the worst part is all the unanswered questions. Why was he out there? Why walk along the canal in the middle of the night? And the drinking? Fraco never drank alcohol." Davet grabbed a wildflower, picking the petals one by one and flinging them violently away from him. "I'll never know… and some nights I just lie in bed torturing myself with how."

With only a brief hesitation, Fie reached out to rest a hand on Davet's knee with a gentle squeeze. Sid gripped his other one. They offered a silent comfort to him.

Twisting around, Davet brought his hands up to take Fie by the head and pulled him in for a kiss, a slightly less chaste version of their first. Davet's tongue flicked across Fie's lips. They broke apart, both breathing heavily.

Before Fie could respond, Davet turned away from him. He caught Sid by the shirt, dragging him closer. Fie had the pleasure of watching their kiss; he tried to calm his body's immediate reaction.

We're not getting naked under the stars on a second date.

Davet sat back on the crate. He rubbed his fingers absently across his lips while glancing between Sid and Fie. "Well?"

"Well?"

Davet shifted his crate as far back as possible. "Aren't you two going to kiss?"

CHAPTER TWENTY-FOUR

DAVET

"Tell me about your date." Simone didn't bother with a hello when Davet finally answered his ringing phone at six in the morning after his night with Sid and Fie. "Well? Are you awake?"

"Barely." Davet shifted the fox off his pillow. He had no idea how Rabbit managed to sneak into his room every night, but his memories of Fraco kept him from trying harder to lock him out. "I haven't had coffee yet."

"I want to know about the kissing." She ranted at him in French while he mostly ignored her. "Are you listening to me?"

"Not really. You know I hate chatting on the phone." Davet put his iPhone on speaker and propped it against a flannel on the bathroom counter. He splashed cold water on his face, trying to wake himself up. "Why don't you bother Jacques?"

"He hangs up."

"What a good idea." Davet fumbled for the towel hanging on a nearby hook. He cringed at the immediately overwhelming sensations from the fuzzy cotton, swiping his face dry and dropping it as quickly as possible before running water over his fingers to try to soothe them. "You couldn't wait for me to wake up and find coffee?"

"You run a coffee shop. How hard do you have to look?"

"Merde. What's the time?" Davet darted around Rabbit, who'd followed him, into the bedroom to find his watch, then belatedly remembered he could've checked his phone. "I ignored my alarm."

"See? Aren't you pleased I called so early?"

"Not really." He made quick work of getting dressed. "Why did you call again?"

"Date. Kissing. Hot sex with your two Brits." Simone laughed, probably at him. Davet didn't feel like asking. "You promised to text me when you got home."

"Sorry." Davet had forgotten. He'd been a bit drunk off kissing. They'd sat under the stars and snogged until his Uncle Santos accidentally on purpose let his dogs out for a midnight walk. "Ils sont parfaits."

"No one is perfect, my sweet."

"Fine, but the kissing definitely had a whiff of perfection." Davet wasn't blind to the faults of the two men, or himself. He made his way through to the kitchen for coffee. "And watching them kiss. Not sure I have enough words in French or English to express how incredible that was."

"I'm coming to visit."

"Excuse me?" Davet dropped his phone in the sink and yanked it out quickly. "Why?"

"Friends visit friends, Davet. We've talked about this before."

He wiped the screen of his phone off on his jeans. "Maybe, but you definitely have an ulterior motive."

"I'm hurt you—"

"No, you aren't. And you can't spend an entire vacation turning me into your live sexual demonstration." Davet banged his hand against the counter, trying to focus himself through the mental whirlwind of Simone visiting, obsessing over whether the date had actually gone as well as he thought, and her teasing. He'd walked the length of the kitchen three times and still forgotten to grab his coffee. "I can't think and talk with you. Bye."

Disconnecting and shoving his phone into his pocket, Davet closed his eyes, breathing in and out to stop his mind from spinning. He repeated one of his favourite lines from a movie. *Rabbit is good, rabbit is wise.* An obscure one, but it made him chuckle given his current furry roommates.

When Davet opened the curtains and large window, he spotted Sid, Fie, and his uncle sitting at one of the picnic tables. Two on one side, with Santos facing them on the other. They all had their arms folded across their chests, studiously avoiding speaking. He topped up his coffee and filled three additional mugs; his morning was definitely about to take a turn, given the glaring going on outside.

Icy stares before eight. Merde. Can I stay inside? Pretend I never saw them? Forever. Probably not.

After feeding the bunny, Davet headed outside with Rabbit following him. He carried a tray out with the four mugs along with a plate of scones. The awkward conversation could happen once he'd inhaled his breakfast.

And coffee.

All of the coffee.

Coffee First.

Too early for bad jokes? Definitely.

"Did you sleep well?" Sid asked in a tone Davet found difficult to decipher. His gaze seemed directed toward Santos, though his question had clearly been for Davet. "Mr Crisp-Ruiz wanted to keep us company while we waited for you to open up."

"Did he?" Davet handed out mugs while Fie grabbed the plate of scones off the tray to set on the middle of the table. "Why are you all acting so stiff and strange?"

"They're taking advantage of you." His uncle pointed at Sid and then Fie with his mug. "They're older, wiser to the world. They...."

Davet watched his uncle struggle to finish his sentence. "They're normal? My brain might be different, but I'm capable of taking care of myself. I'm not a child."

"Isn't it a bit late to turn on your protective instincts? Where were you when your sister and her husband abused Davet and Fraco? Did that not offend your sensibilities?" Fie dropped his truth on Santos with all the finesse of a sledgehammer. "Is it our age, gender, or your own guilty conscience bringing out this new side?"

"Fie." Sid placed a hand on his shoulder. Davet glanced toward him in surprise at his being the voice of reason over Fie, who usually seemed the calmer of the two. "What happened to keeping our noses out of their family issues?"

"He put their family issues in our face with this ridiculous posturing." Fie shrugged. He took an angry bite of scone. "I changed my mind when he acted as though we'd stolen Davet's virginity, which we haven't. How long have you known me, Santos? And Sid? Why've you suddenly decided we belong on a most wanted list of evil villains?"

For a brief moment, Davet considered filming the argument for entertainment purposes. He knew his auntie and Simone would both enjoy a viewing. His mood plummeted a little with the implications of his uncle's accusations.

Trouble was, Davet thought Fie had a point. Santos had picked his moments to play protective uncle. In his mind, it was quite a number of years too late for the gesture to feel genuine.

Why now?

Was age the issue?

Sid and Fie had quite a few years on Davet, and many people looked askance at age differences. Or was Santos bothered by three men being in a relationship? None of the potential answers comforted him.

"Drink your coffee." Davet had to repeat himself several times until all three men stopped speaking over each other and him. "Perhaps my opinion on *my* sex life matters more than anyone else's?"

He received three affirmative responses, though his uncle's response was muted. The sudden overprotective streak was incredibly confusing.

I could've used his interventions years ago as a kid when I had zero control over my life. He's too late.

"Davet."

He held a hand up to silence his uncle. "Fie's right. You're more vocal in my defence than you were six months ago at the funeral. Is it guilt?"

"Of course not," Santos snapped. "I love you. You're family."

"I was family then—and six years ago. Is there a special reason you found the ability to speak up now?" Davet hid the trembling in his fingers by gripping his mug tightly. He hated confrontation; his entire body screamed for him to run into the cottage and slam the door on them. "You trusted Sid and Fie for years. Called them heroes. You even told me to count on them."

"They are heroes."

Davet hunched his shoulders, trying to ease the tension building in his body. "Then what is it? I don't understand. I'm not a virgin to be sequestered away from any potential threat to my innocence. What sort of repressed nonsense is that?"

Stopping his rant when his uncle choked on his coffee, Davet waited patiently for him to regain control and mop up the mess on his shirt. He refused to be treated as a child or even a teenager. Why dance around the topic of sex?

I'm a consenting adult.

What's there to be ashamed of?

"I haven't seen them naked—yet," Davet added helpfully. Santos didn't appear reassured by the clarification. "Listen, I don't see a problem. Customers should be showing up within the next hour or so. Can we not waste more time on a subject that isn't any of your business?"

"Morning." His auntie walked up and squeezed on the bench between Davet and her husband. "Now, are we all playing nicely?"

"No." Davet readily threw his uncle under the bus. "Uncle Santos has decided to inject himself into my sexual escapades."

Santos spewed coffee across the table. "Could you not?"

Grabbing his mug and the empty plate, Davet left his aunt to sort her husband out. He'd had enough for one day. Puttering around in the kitchen, he decided to pretend they weren't outside to avoid obsessing about the muffled conversation.

A buzz from his phone jolted him out of trying to eavesdrop on them. *Jacques.* Davet found a text mentioning a little bird had told his ex-lover about kissing. Simone, unfortunately, had a tendency to gossip with Jacques.

Why did I introduce them?

Jacques: How is your morning after?
Davet: Ugh.
Jacques: Something wrong?
Davet: Family being family.

Ending the text chat with Jacques, Davet steeled his nerves for a long morning. Most days he barely managed to get through his early rush of customers before needing a break from people. With the drama and tension, it would take a miracle to avoid a meltdown.

To hold off the inevitable, Davet brought his laptop into the kitchen and turned on one of his favourite programmes. He hoped to soothe his nerves a little. His regulars might be understanding, but he hated meltdowns.

They left him exhausted and incapable of functioning.

"You all right?" Sid stepped up to the open window. "Shirley dropped off her baskets of goodies. I promised to make sure they arrived safely."

Davet waved him toward the door, taking the

baskets to set up on the counter. He noticed one of the covers wasn't sitting flush on top. "Did you nick one? Should I report a theft?"

"What's the price of silence?" Sid brushed off crumbs from his shirt.

"A kiss."

Sid stepped closer, backing Davet up against the cabinet behind him. He gripped the counter on either side, which left Davet in a prison of his arms. "Just one?"

"One for me as well." Fie joined them in the kitchen, closing the door behind him. He smiled at both of them. "Then we can help you set up for the day."

Or distract me.

CHAPTER TWENTY-FIVE

SID

"Can I help you?" Sid had been preparing to take a quick break when Jacinda positioned herself in his doorway. "I'm going out."

"No." Jacinda blocked his office door, refusing to allow him to leave. "I'm saving you from yourself. Davet won't appreciate you verbally flaying his uncle. You've been brooding in here for the last few days."

"Did you watch *Game of Thrones* again? Who uses flaying anymore?" Sid's annoyance with Santos had simmered for a few days after their uncomfortable morning coffee. His pot, as Fie's mum would've said, had finally boiled over. "We're going to have a friendly chat."

"Then you won't mind if I tag along?" She stubbornly ignored his attempts to gently shove her out of the way. "To make sure it stays friendly."

"Fine. You're buying coffee." He grabbed his keys.

"And you're not allowed to record the conversation."

"Spoilsport." Jacinda waved a paper with a list of coffees on it. "You are buying because you lost the betting pool on the season."

"Fuck. I forgot."

Every year, they got together to pick the top three and the relegation three of the Premier League. The loser had to buy coffee for all the detectives. Not once, nor twice, but for an entire week. Sid had put off punishment for months, mostly by dodging into the loo when Jacinda came calling with her order list.

"Don't be a sore loser—or a liar. You haven't forgotten." She followed him out to the car park, leaning against the vehicle next to his. "Are you serious about Fie and Davet?"

Sid resisted the urge to snap out an immediate answer. "I'm not asking them to marry me."

"Deflection? Already? It's a bit early," Jacinda teased gently. "People will talk about you. Three men in a relationship."

"Are you getting in?" Sid got into the driver side, giving himself time to consider his answer. "I don't care what people say."

"Really?" She paused in the process of pulling on her seat belt. "You're a police detective. Not everyone is kind or open-minded about relationships, even though the world has become less judgemental."

"Has it?" Sid had seen the best and worst of the world as a member of the armed forces and now as a police officer. "We can weather the storm. Stop distracting me from my purpose."

They bickered like siblings the rest of the way across the village. Sid parked at the coffee shop, leaving Jacinda to talk coffee with Davet. He disappeared across the field to find Santos.

"Sidney." Santos eyed him suspiciously when Sid wandered into the garden and found him working in his shed. "You're a day late if you're planning to tell me off."

"Fie beat me to it?"

"My wife."

Sid almost felt sorry for him. He sat on a wooden stool and watched Santos work. "We'd never hurt Davet."

"Not on purpose." Santos gripped the sander in his hand before setting it off to the side. "Davet doesn't always understand. He can't read your expression or tone of voice. You could easily break his heart despite your best intentions."

"Being autistic doesn't make him incapable of maintaining a romantic relationship." Sid had never appreciated how frustrating the coddling must be for Davet before now. He'd be extra cognisant going forward to avoid being yet another hurdle for him to overcome. "You seem to be the one having issues with understanding the situation. He's an adult. Back the fuck off and let him be one."

"I'm trying."

"Try harder." Sid had come to the conclusion that if Davet was able to function in a non-autistic world, they could at least make an effort to meet him halfway. "And seriously, sulking in the shed isn't helping anyone."

"I'm not sulking." Santos pointed a piece of stained wood at him. "Davet asked for a fox door so Rabbit can go out in the morning on his own."

"A fox door?" Sid snorted in amusement.

Since Fraco's death, Sid had noticed Davet going above and beyond for the animals left behind. The rabbit and fox had become almost representations of his little brother for him. It was at least a healthy coping mechanism.

"I'm sorry."

Sid shook himself out of his thoughts. "Not sure I'm the one who truly deserves to hear your apology. I accept on my behalf."

"I'll chat with Davet." Santos grasped the subtle hint Sid had directed his way. "Just be careful with him, yeah?"

Honestly.

Deciding not to waste his breath, Sid made his way through the field to the little cottage that housed Coffee First. He didn't know if they'd actually made any progress with Santos. He might always see his nephew as a person in need of protection.

In Sid's opinion, guilt lay at the heart of the issue for Santos. He might never fully forgive himself for not rescuing his nephews as children. Davet would likely always have a small amount of resentment over the issue.

Can't say I blame him either.

"Is he alive?" Jacinda had a mug in one hand and a pastry in the other. "Davet's making your coffee now."

"I decided not to heap insult onto injury seeing as he'd already been whipped into submission by a stronger person." Sid grinned at her before stealing the rest of her pastry. "Have you gotten our orders in? We do have work to do."

"Not going to sneak a snog in now?"

Sid had no doubts Davet wouldn't appreciate being the object of attention from all of his customers. "No, because public displays of affection while on the job are generally frowned upon."

"You sound like my mother." Jacinda shuddered. "I will pay you to never do it again. Go and say hello and get our coffees while you're in there. We're going to be late for the mid-morning briefing."

"Bugger." Sid glanced at his watch to find he'd dithered at the shed with Santos longer than anticipated. "I'm blaming you."

"Typical."

After a quick hello to Davet and an even faster kiss while hidden behind the door, Sid grabbed the coffees for his fellow detectives. Davet balanced a bag with pastries on top, waving cheerfully when Sid grumbled at him. Jacinda kindly opened the door for him but failed to help carry the drinks.

"You could help."

"I could." Jacinda trailed after him. "But it's good for you to struggle occasionally."

"I told you to stop reading the fortunes in those cookies." Sid glanced pointedly from the car door over his shoulder at Jacinda. "My Hogwarts letter never arrived, so alohamora is out. Are you planning on walking to the station?"

"Fine, fine." She took the drinks holder from him. "Hurry up."

Coffee and pastries lasted all of a minute during their briefing. Sid headed to his office with a new case in hand. He paused just outside when he spotted a familiar figure waiting for him.

"I can see you standing there."

Sid tapped his fingers against his cup and forced his legs to carry him into the office. He sat across from his father. *Here's hoping the conversation goes better than last time.* "Did you get lost again?"

"I wasn't lost the first time." His father sat stiffly across from him. "Can we talk?"

Sid stared mournfully at his empty cup. *Will anyone notice if I exchange whisky for coffee?* "Again? We did so brilliantly the last time."

"I dreamt your mother refused to talk to me in heaven for how I'd treated her baby boy," he admitted. "I do love you, son."

You've a funny way of showing it, don't you?

Sid restrained his urge to be callously narky. "Is this

an apology?"

It's a shit one. Then again, when did dad ever apologise to anyone who wasn't mum?

Never.

Little men had large egos. Sid had heard repeatedly in his teens his gran and his mum complain about their husbands being big-headed. He'd inherited the stubbornness that came with being too prideful for his own good.

His saving grace had been military service. Nothing knocked the arrogance out of a person like crawling through mud. Sid had always believed being part of a team made him a better person.

And humbled him.

A little.

"Are you willing to give me a chance?"

"At what?" Sid wanted to be clear on what his father hoped for in the future. "I never closed the door, Dad. You slammed it in my face."

"And I'm sorry." His father leaned forward in his chair. "Can you forgive me?"

CHAPTER TWENTY-SIX

Fie

"Is it time for a walk?" Fie had been sketching out ideas for new mugs when Haggard brought a lead over to him.

Double checking the kiln, Fie headed outside into the afternoon sun with Haggard. The weather had been beautiful the last few days. He intended to enjoy every moment before the rains inevitably returned.

And they would.

"Where are you going?" Fie stumbled slightly when Haggard bumped into his legs.

When Haggard led Fie through a field outside of the village, he didn't expect to find both Sid and Davet. The former was on his back with a book covering his face. The latter had been writing in a journal with both the fox and rabbit near him.

"Is this what you wanted me to find?" Fie reached down to pet Haggard. They continued forward until

Davet spotted him. "Can I join you?"

Haggard huffed at him.

"Sorry, can we join you?" Fie narrowed his eyes on Haggard, who collapsed next to Rabbit. The dog and fox had apparently become friends. "Swear he understands every bloody word out of my mouth."

Sid lifted his hand to wave but didn't bother moving. "Swayze."

"Shouldn't you be chasing villains and rescuing kittens from trees?" He sat between the two, wondering what had happened. Sid's voice sounded flat. "What happened?"

"His father apologised." Davet paused in his writing and shifted the bunny in his lap slightly. "He doesn't know how to accept while still being angry."

"Succinct and accurate." Sid rolled on his side, letting the book fall away. "I told my father I'd think about it. And now I feel like the biggest wanker in history."

"Why?" Fie didn't know, if roles were reversed, if he'd feel overly forgiving either. "You didn't slam the figurative door in his face."

Flopping on his back again, Sid recovered his face with the book. *Conversation over then?* Fie glanced over to find Davet had gotten lost in his writing.

They'd discovered Davet enjoyed writing as a hobby. Not stories or poems. He journaled his thoughts and conversation to help process them. Fie found himself sitting in the relative silence, enjoying an impromptu date.

"Did anyone bring tea?" Sid had never handled lengthy silences well. "I'm starved. Does Domino's deliver to fields?"

"Pizza or tea?" Fie nudged Sid with his foot.

"Both. Maybe not at the same time." He sat up, brushing grass from his trousers. "How about we pick up a pizza and eat at your place?"

"Why mine?"

"Davet lives in a tin can and my place isn't much better. You've got space—and a bigger telly." Sid caught Rabbit when the fox darted past him. "Davet?"

Davet jolted as if being woken from a dream. "What?"

"Date night in with pizza and whatever's on the telly?" Sid asked.

"It's the afternoon." Davet closed his journal, capped his pen, and stowed both in a small pocket of the satchel that he placed his rabbit into for safe passage. "We're early for supper."

"I'm a growing lad." Sid patted his belly.

"Is that normal at your age? Don't men usually stop growing in their twenties?" Davet sounded completely confused. "Oh, right, joking."

"Are you interested in pizza or would you rather we left you alone for the evening?" Fie knew Davet frequently hid away after a day of running his coffee shop. "We'd miss you, but understand if you've reached a limit of being social."

Davet appeared taken back by their willingness to adjust plans based on his mood. "No anchovies. Weird, fishy, not pizza food."

Fie couldn't argue with the assessment. "Sid?"

"Was I wrong?"

"About anchovies?" Davet got to his feet and called Rabbit the not-bunny over to him from where he'd been playing with Haggard. "Have I gotten confused again?"

"No, you haven't. He changed subjects midsentence." Fie reached down to drag Sid to his feet. "And no, MacFluff, you weren't wrong to ask for time from your dad. He denied you, then came back expecting to be immediately embraced."

"He can. He's old." Sid trudged alongside him as Fie led the way through the field towards his cottage. "I couldn't look him in the eye and accept his apology. How could I when he threw me away?"

"Maybe you just need time to process?" Davet had caught up to them after his rabbit hopped out of the bag. "Forgiveness doesn't happen in an instant. He's had time to adjust to wanting to speak with you again, and the least he can do is allow you space to do the same."

"He's right." Fie tried to ignore the twinge in his chest when he considered his own family. Would they forgive him for withdrawing from them? Was suffering from post-traumatic stress enough of an excuse? "Your dad can't demand you accept his apology when he wants."

Heartbreaks don't heal on demand.
Mine certainly took forever.

CHAPTER TWENTY-SEVEN

Davet

Pizza led to them camped out on the living room floor arguing over the best way to win at Uno. Sid and Fie had a rather aggressive manner of playing. Davet imagined their version wasn't far off the exploding snap game from Harry Potter.

The only thing we're missing is fireworks.
Who takes Uno seriously?

"He cheats." Sid pointed his pizza crust at Fie. He definitely took Uno more seriously than Davet thought possible. "Not sure how, but he does."

"Magic." Fie gathered up the cards to set them on the coffee table they'd shoved out of the way. "I don't need to cheat, you've never been lucky at cards."

"And you've rotten luck when it comes to love." Sid tossed the crust into the pizza box. "What time is it? I've got an early morning shift to cover because Jacinda decided to fob it off on me."

Somehow, between the pizza and games, Davet had felt the energy in the room change slowly. *Have we reached the kissing stage of the evening?* He'd spent all afternoon reminding himself Sid was too upset for a kiss.

When Fie had joined them, Davet had hoped things would take a turn for the better. Sid's mood had slowly lifted. *How do I bring up the kissing?*

Merde.

Why is this so hard?

Annoyed with his own inability to bring up intimacy, Davet ripped apart the paper with their scores. He left a pile of confetti on the carpet. Starting anything had always been difficult for him; all the negative possibilities of rejection sent his mind into a whirlwind of anxiety.

The mound of confetti debris grew in front of Davet. Fie didn't do anything more than raise his eyebrows a little. He offered a stack of papers to him if he needed additional stress relief.

It was a lovely gesture that only helped to make Davet feel as if they were watching him panic. *Yes, there's nothing quite so relaxing as being stared at during a meltdown.* He continued to rip the Nando's menu.

Davet fidgeted a while longer before deciding he'd have to be the one to make the first move. "How do you feel about condoms?"

Merde.

One of these days I'll manage not to say the first thought in my mind. Why haven't they said anything? Can you die of embarrassment? I'm definitely halfway into the grave.

Who just blurts out a question about condoms?

Me.

I do.

"Condoms in general or for a specific purpose?" Fie recovered enough to ask.

"Uh." Davet's mind went blank. He found himself incapable of formulating a coherent response behind a grunt. "I…."

Not now.

Please, not now.

Fie stretched a hand across to pat him on the leg. "Take your time. We're not in a hurry."

Trying to avoid his mind shutting down never worked. Davet had to ride the wave of silence out as always. He was capable of talking, but his brain usually refused to process anything beyond a yes or no.

Davet couldn't imagine a more humiliating way to end a date. His thoughts continued to slip away from him before reaching his tongue. "I'm…."

"You enjoy James Bond movies, right? Fie's got them on DVD. How about we put one on and see if your words come back to you eventually?" Sid tossed the remote over to Fie and got up to hunt through his collection of movies. "Conversation will hold until you're ready."

Their kind acceptance made him emotional, which didn't help much. Davet slowly stopped attempting to bury himself under the paper. He reminded himself repeatedly his struggle didn't make him any less desirable of a partner.

I'm not broken or a puzzle for them to solve.

I can do this—it might just be a bit different from what they've experienced before.

They made it through one and a half Bond films before Davet finally began to relax. He sat up slightly, gathering up the massive amount of paper debris. Fie held out the empty pizza box for him to throw the rubbish into.

"Condoms." Davet snickered when Sid almost dropped his mug of tea. "I'm particular about them. A texture sensitivity thing. I can't— Not without one."

"We don't mind," Sid rushed to assure him. "Condoms, lube, feathers, leather, grass. Well, I might have to consider the grass."

"Grass?" Davet tried to figure out what he meant.

"MacFluff." Fie flicked Sid on the leg to stop him from laughing. "He's not wrong, though. Condoms aren't going to be an issue for either of us. Whatever you need to be comfortable."

Their kisses, over the past few dates, had grown increasingly carnal, a far cry from the innocent peck Davet had given them that day on the beach after the funeral. For all their similarities, Sid and Fie had drastically different approaches.

Sid had zero hesitancy. His kisses were brash and plundering in a way Davet thought only existed in romantic novels and fan fiction. He tended to take great pleasure in reducing Davet and Fie to breathless panting.

On the other end of the pleasurable kissing spectrum, Fie lingered possessively over both of them. His lips repeatedly brushed until Davet had to open his mouth for more. Fie took his time with a demanding slowness that brought both of his partners to their knees with desire.

Despite their earlier conversations, Fie had made certain both Davet and Sid wanted to move forward. Consent mattered to him—as it should. Davet found his insistence on clear communication sweet and comforting.

"Help him undress, Sid." Fie leaned against the side of the couch after clearing everything off the rug. "Nice and slow."

One thing became crystal clear quickly: Fie enjoyed being in control. He directed them around easily, and Davet, for the first time, could see how he'd managed to take charge of a group of soldiers. *Though probably not sexually. Oh, now there's a dream for another day.*

Davet found breathing steadily nigh impossible with calloused fingers stripping off his T-shirt and cargo shorts. He'd skipped briefs because of the heat, which now seemed even more convenient with Sid taking advantage of every bare inch of skin. "Fie."

Their conductor shifted closer to them. Davet reached out to catch him by the shirt and slid his hands underneath. His fingers traced the lines of scars he found along Fie's upper body.

They explored each other's bodies, leaving clothing haphazardly strewn about the room. Sid propped himself up on the couch, drawing Davet over to straddle his body. Fie reached between them to wrap his hand around their hard shafts, stroking them while the three traded sloppy kisses.

Shifting behind him, Fie pressed Davet between them. He kissed along Davet's neck then leaned around to brush his lips against Sid's. They continued to trade back and forth.

Fie slid his cock along Davet's back with his hand still sliding over their shafts. Sid's fingers drifted up to tease Davet's nipples. "This is going to be brilliant."

"Condoms." Davet shuddered between them. He didn't want to risk sensation overload ruining their first time together. "Now, please."

"Right." Fie rubbed against him a few more times before getting to his feet. "Condoms. Where the bloody hell did I put them?"

"I hid them in your old Weetabix box," Sid muttered after a moment.

"Do I even want to know why in the Weetabix?" Fie rolled his eyes and then made his way into the kitchen. "We're going to chat about boundaries after this."

"Your cock is going to be in me, and you want to

natter on about boundaries?" Sid winked at Davet, who didn't quite understand the byplay between them. "He's had the same box of Weetabix in his cupboard for a year; I wanted to know how long it took him to find the condoms."

Davet didn't get the prank even after the explanation, but his mind was happily focused on the glide of his cock against Sid's. He'd continued to rock himself while they waited for Fie. "Hard to focus on figuring out what you're talking about when you keep...." His words trailed off into nothing when Fie returned, walked up to them to grip Sid by the hair, and fed his cock into his mouth. Davet had a perfect view. He couldn't look away from them

After several minutes, Fie pulled away from them. He tossed the box of condoms on the floor beside Sid and knelt on the rug. They both turned toward Davet. A thrill of anticipation ran along his spine.

The raw energy of touch and sound threatened to disrupt his enjoyment. Davet had to focus on moments to keep his mind from spinning out of control trying to take everything in. He found an amazing balance between the three of them; no one was left out in the cold to simply watch.

"I've always wanted to christen this rug." Sid rolled over on his hands and knees, glancing over his shoulder to wink at them. "Well?"

Davet laughed when Sid did an incredibly awkward twerk. "Are we taking turns?"

Grabbing him by the wrist, Sid dragged Davet underneath him. He shook the box of condoms until several fell onto the rug. Fie grabbed one as well, along with a bottle of lube, which hadn't been in the cereal box but in the drawer where he usually kept them.

The next hour went by in the blur that good sex always was for Davet. He struggled to lose himself in the pleasure of hands, fingers, and tongues when his brain wanted to pick each moment apart. He knew from past experience that ruined the moment.

Pleasure involved intense focus for him.

Sid and Fie certainly seemed driven to allow him all the focus required.

And holy hell, is he driving into me.

As the middle of their delicious sandwich, Davet seesawed between Fie behind him and Sid in front. He rested his forehead against Sid's back while squeezing a hand underneath to stroke his cock, rocking his hips in a perfect rhythm. His attention tunnelled down to just the gradually building explosion.

Sid went first, carrying Davet with him. The squeezing around him was too much for his body to handle. Intense pleasure short-circuited his mind. He blinked and found himself almost crushed against Sid by Fie, who'd obviously been taken along with them.

"Can you lot get off me? You fucking weigh a ton," Sid groaned from underneath their boneless pile. "I am not into asphyxiation."

Fie eased out of Davet and helped them both get up.

"Toss your condom in here."

Davet ignored the rubbish bin Fie held out to him. He ducked into the loo to have a quick wash, returning to find the two men on the rug. Sid grabbed his arm to drag him down between them. Davet couldn't help a slightly self-conscious query. "Good, right?"

"Brilliant." Sid huffed. "I'd kiss you, but I think you two broke my ribs."

As they lay collapsed on their backs on the floor, Davet didn't think any of them would be moving for a while. He'd never been so thoroughly and blissfully exhausted.

A knock on the door had them all jolting up to stare wildly at each other.

"Sod it all." Fie tripped over Sid trying to get up and grab his trousers. Davet sat up, pressing his lips together to keep from laughing. "Where the hell are my boxers?"

"Here." Sid tugged them out from underneath his body and tossed them over. "You could always pretend you aren't home."

"Can't. Your vehicle is outside. If we don't answer, someone is going to start to worry about us. What if it's Jane? She can pick a lock in a second. I'd rather be dressed." Fie rushed to get into his jeans and shirt. The latter went on inside out as well as backwards. "Put your clothes on while I see who it is."

They took longer to get dressed because Sid kept dragging him over for a kiss. Davet had learnt that Sid tended to be more tactile than Fie. He did eventually manage to get his cargo shorts and T-shirt on as angry voices drifted over from the front door.

"Bugger." Sid hopped up quickly, shoving his feet into his shoes without bothering with socks. "I'd know that voice anywhere."

After taking an extra moment to dress properly, Davet made his way to the front of the cottage. He crowded behind Sid to peek around and find Fie mid-argument with another man. It became obvious after a few seconds it was Fie's ex.

"Oh, look, it's Edmund." Sid shifted to the side to allow Davet to step between them. "Have any Turkish Delight lately?"

"What?" Edmund paused in the middle of his argument with Fie to frown at Sid. "You. What are you doing here?"

"Being fucked by the man you dumped. His cock's brilliant. No idea why you left him. Have a good evening." Sid pushed both Fie and Davet into the house then slammed the door shut in Edmund's face. "Anyone else starving? Did we eat all the pizza?"

Fie pinched the bridge of his nose when the doorbell rang again. He grabbed Sid as he went to open it. "Leave him alone. I'm not stooping to his level."

"Why is he even here?" Sid asked.

"I've apparently been ignoring his phone calls and text messages. He decided a second visit might change my mind." Fie shrugged indifferently. "Not interested in discussing Edmund further."

Davet didn't see a point in inserting himself into drama from a previous relationship. "Do you have anything edible aside from Weetabix?"

"Not sure the Weetabix is edible." Sid opened the door when Fie turned away, and loomed over Edmund, who'd continued to ring the bell and knock as well. "What do you want? He's not interested in you."

"It's none of your—"

Sid seemed close to wanting to punch the man. Davet thought a detective physically assaulting someone was probably frowned on. He placed a hand on Sid's arm to hopefully keep him from attacking. "He fell apart, and we could only watch. How the hell do you get off breaking a heart then swanning back in as if nothing happened?"

"Fie?" Edmund glanced between the three men, then over to his ex.

Davet stepped in front of Sid to sneer at the man. "Weakness. I see weakness in you. I've no doubts Fie would've seen through you even without the heartbreak of being dumped. Go home, wherever that is. Think about the beautiful bear of a man who has the greatest heart—"

"And cock," Sid interrupted.

"Yes, that too," Davet agreed. He easily dismissed Edmund without bothering to finish his sentence, returning to the house and leaving the others to wrap the conversation up. "I'm starved."

I suppose I don't have to worry about Fie's ex-boyfriend.

At all.

They decided not to tempt fate with either the pizza or Weetabix. Davet whipped up a large omelette with onions, cheese, and bacon. Sid managed the toast without burning it while Fie cleaned up their mess from the living room.

Food, sex, more food.

This is definitely the start of something wonderful.

CHAPTER TWENTY-EIGHT

Sid

Breakfast came with a side of bacon and a quickie in bed. Sid thanked Fie's foresight in getting a Caesar, apparently the largest bed available. They'd slept squashed together easily.

At least Sid and Fie had slept squashed together. Davet had started between them and wound up stretched across the foot of the mattress. He couldn't get comfortable without some space to himself.

And I pegged him as the little spoon.
That's what I get for judging a book by its size.
What the hell am I thinking about?

He'd headed into the police station in a far better mood than usual for five in the morning. Coffee, a good English breakfast, and sex did wonders for his mood. His brilliant day evaporated not long after getting to his desk.

"Sid? Have you got a minute?" Dave waved a sticky

note at him. "Call came in about a missing grandmother. The son lives in Dublin. Can you do a welfare check? Make sure she's all right. It's Mrs. Knight. I'm sure she forgot to charge her phone."

"Why me? She always pinches my arse when I go check on her." Sid grabbed the paper from a grinning Dave and grumbled all the way to his vehicle.

One of their more eccentric residents, Mrs Knight, had lived in Bideford for the majority of her life. Her husband had died a few years back and her children lived elsewhere. At least once a month, one of them called asking for the police to ensure she hadn't fallen.

She was always fine. They'd have a cup of tea with her while she showed photos of her grandkids for the hundredth time. And inevitably, Sid's bum got pinched.

"Should've worn padding." Sid checked his reflection in the rearview mirror. He rubbed absently at the reddened mark on his neck. *How the hell did I miss the massive love bite?* "I wonder if I can get away with a scarf in the middle of summer."

Thanking his lucky stars Jacinda had the day off, Sid drove the short distance across town to the little cottage Mrs Knight called home. He hated to wake her so early in the morning. His repeated knocks went unnoticed, but what worried him more was that her yappy little Yorkie hadn't barked once.

"Shit." Sid grabbed his radio to call into the station. "Dave?"

"How's the bottom?"

"She's not answering her door. Neither is the dog." Sid crouched down to peer into the letterbox. He tried yelling through the opening to get her attention. "Mrs Knight? Can you hear me in there? It's Detective Inspector Little. Your son rang us because you didn't answer his calls."

"Nothing?"

"Not even a whisper." He tried the door handle without luck. "Dave, you might want to send me some help. Not sure if I'm going to be able to get in without breaking a window. She might need medical attention as well."

"Already on it."

Sid made his way along the cottage to the garden gate. He had to stretch an arm over the top to unlatch the lock. His uneasy feeling increased tenfold when he came around the side of the home. "The back door is open."

"Broken?"

"Not that I can see." Sid bent down to check the doorframe as well as the lock. "Maybe she went for a walk?"

He shook his head even as the words came out of his mouth. Mrs Knight hadn't left her door open. She might forget to charge her phone or pay her bills on occasion, but she'd been almost obsessive about locking up.

Despite his instincts to rush inside, Sid waited for the familiar sound of an ambulance. They'd lucked out with paramedics not being all that far from the house. Dave kept him updated unnecessarily given Sid could hear sirens.

"Detective Inspector Little?"

Sid stood up to greet the paramedics and additional officers who'd responded to Dave's radio call. "Morning."

"Where's our patient?" Victoria had worked with Sid several times. "Is she all right?"

"Let's see if we can find her." Sid made his way into the house. They didn't have to go far to find her. Mrs Knight lay in her kitchen with a shattered cup of tea beside her. She looked as though she'd just opened the door for her pet to go out. "Dave? Get a hold of her family, will you? They'll want to come home. And I've got a feeling her dog is on the loose."

Leaving Mrs Knight in the capable and respectful hands of the paramedics, Sid organised several of the officers around to join him on a cursory search for the dog. They were likely too late for his owner, but maybe they could save her furry companion.

How many coppers does it take to corral one small creature?

The correct answer turned out to be all available, and they didn't find the dog anyway. One of the village kids recognised him while walking her own dog and brought him to Mrs Knight's cottage.

Thankfully, someone caught her before she made her way to the front door. They didn't need a traumatised eleven-year-old on top of everything else. Sid now had an armful of Yorkie to handle.

Think he'd make a decent rug?

After a few calls, Dave managed to get one of their local veterinarians on the phone. Sid dropped the Yorkie off. They'd watch over him until Mrs Knight's family arrived.

All the blissfully relaxed energy from the morning had completely evaporated. Sid didn't want to return to the cottage. He had a job to do, though, so he made his way back over to speak with the coroner who'd been called in by the paramedics.

Mrs Knight had already been removed from her cottage. They didn't have the official report. Unofficially, the coroner believed her death had been from natural causes.

Old age.

What a terrible determination to make about the death of a person.

They died of old age.

Sid found himself painfully reminded of his father's visits in recent days. "Right. I'm heading back to the office."

"Yes, sir."

Nodding to the young officer who'd been left to watch the house until the family arrived, Sid trudged over to his vehicle. He considered picking up lunch, but his appetite hadn't made an appearance yet. *What if I'd checked on Mrs Knight earlier?*

Why didn't we make a routine of visiting her? Or someone else?

Starved but without an appetite, Sid hid at his desk. A preliminary report from the coroner mocked him from his inbox. *How long was she lying on her floor, alone, dying?*

Sid had always believed in doing his best to help everyone. He had a hero complex that drove him to be a better detective and a human being. "Make a plan to fix things. To do something for others in the village."

"You might start with not nattering to yourself in your office." Jacinda stepped inside holding a bag from Nando's. "So, our Dave texted me while I was out on my day off. I thought you might enjoy a bit of greasy goodness. Lift your spirits."

The enticing scent of spices and chips had Sid's taste buds salivating. He offered a grateful grin before snatching the bag from her. Jacinda flopped into one of the spare chairs across his desk, lifting up the second container of Nando's for herself.

"Sidney Little." She leaned forward in the seat, staring intently at him. "Has someone gnawed on your neck recently? A vampire perhaps?"

Sid bit into one of the chicken wings, chewing slowly to avoid answering. He forced his shoulders down when he hunched up instinctually to block her view. "Mrs Knight's family should be here either this evening or tomorrow. Her son's a surgeon, apparently, and had to get another doctor to cover for him."

"Sidney."

"Jacinda," he retorted, mimicking her inflexion perfectly.

"Did someone finally scratch your itch?" She cheered when he couldn't stop the grin from spreading across his face. "Was it Fie or Davet?"

"Both."

"Little?" Their sergeant poked her head into his office. "You've a visitor at the front desk."

"Sorry, Jacinda. You'll have to wait for the juicy gossip. Don't eat all my chips." Sid grabbed a napkin to wipe his hands and face clean. He strode down the hall and through the door to find his father waiting once again by the front desk. "Afternoon."

"Can we talk?"

With Mrs Knight's lonely death fresh in his mind, Sid found a new perspective on his personal family drama. He led his father through to his office, where Jacinda promptly absconded with her lunch to give them privacy. She did pop back in a few minutes later with cups of tea for them both.

Altruistic, or a bribe to get me to gossip about my night?

Definitely a bribe.

"Mind if I eat?" Sid grabbed the abandoned Nando's sack. One bite had only served to wake up his appetite. "I've had an agonisingly exhausting day and it's not even tea time yet. Let's not dance around the issue again. You want to compromise, but I refuse to pretend to be straight. I won't hide my love of men to make you comfortable. No relationship can survive that nonsense. Not for long."

"Can't you avoid—"

"All or nothing. I'm either your son, or I'm not." Sid tried not to laugh at the absurdity of making such serious ultimatums while pointing a half-eaten chicken wing at his dad. "My life doesn't work in a closet. Shouldn't you want me to be happy and leading a fulfilled life?"

"I do."

Sid lowered the chicken wing and searched his father's face. He seemed older, more wrinkles, and exhausted. Had Mrs Knight wanted her children closer? "Why don't you have supper with a couple of friends and me?"

"Just friends?"

No, we're fuck buddies.

"We might be more than friends." Sid wondered if maybe he should've talked with Davet and Fie about his idea first. "If you can act like a decent human being, maybe this will work."

And if you can't, I won't sacrifice my happiness.
Not again.

CHAPTER TWENTY-NINE

FIE

The cottage smelled different.

Not bad, just different.

On bad nights where memories hit hard, Fie had taken to straightening up his cottage. As a result, it usually smelled of cleaning products. After only one night, Sid and Davet had brought warmth into his home.

To his surprise, Haggard even seemed to miss them. He'd sat by the door for a while after both Sid and Davet had rushed off to work. How had one night together magnified his loneliness to such an extent?

For so long, Fie had remained withdrawn from his friends and family. A strange numbness had settled over him. A single evening and morning with them had melted away part of his icy wall of protection.

Fie had intended to spend his day working on mugs when Jacinda rang. "Did you get the wrong number?"

"Yes, I looked in my list of contacts for the 'beary mug maker' and accidentally selected you," Jacinda responded with her usual snark. "Are you busy?"

"Yes."

"Staring at your mug of coffee isn't work. Hold on."

Fie listened to her muffled yelling for a few seconds before she returned. "I'm not busy. Did you need something?"

"Mrs Knight passed away." Jacinda got right to the point and took Fie's breath away with her bluntness. "Sid went out to check on her; they found her in the kitchen. Can't tell you much more, obviously, but he's not taking it well."

"And?"

"Given the size of the bite on his neck, I thought you might want to know how his mood is." Jacinda sounded far too amused for Fie's liking. "I'm worried. I brought him Nando's, but his father, arse that he is, showed up."

After the call ended, Fie found himself thinking about poor Mrs Knight. He'd made mugs especially for her. They were lighter than normal as her fingers had trouble holding regular ones.

She'd been a lovely woman who loved her dog. Fie wondered how her children felt knowing she'd passed away on her own. *Devastated and guilty.* His thoughts turned toward his own parents. His mum reached out constantly to him, sending packages of baked treats, probably hoping to get some sort of response.

Fie held his mobile in his hand for several long seconds.

Am I pushing myself too fast?

Too fast?

I'm a damned glacier, given how many years have gone by without reaching out.

Time to stop being such an arsehole.

He scrolled through his contact list and hit Send on a number he hadn't dialled in ages, waiting patiently for the familiar, cheerful "Hullo." His eyes welled up with tears, and Haggard moved over to sit beside him. "Mum."

"Morogh." She paused, and he heard her breath catch. "Are you done hiding now, love?"

"Mum." Fie couldn't get much else out when his throat clogged with emotion. He reached behind him blindly and caught a chair to drag over, sitting before his legs went out from underneath him. "I…."

"Can we come and visit now?"

Fie had suddenly become incapable of formulating a sentence. "I'm—"

"Wonderful. I'll talk to your father. We'll be down in a twinkling." She disconnected before Fie had a chance to speak again.

"Damn it."

I've made a large family-sized mistake.

Fie glared at his phone for betraying him. His mum was probably talking to every single member of his family. A mass migration from Scotland had probably already begun.

Because they needed his mad relatives to mingle with Sid's not-so-pleasant father if they ever got together, the only thing missing from the group was Davet's parents showing up again. He supposed they should be pleased his family tended to welcome all. His mum might even manage to beat Sid's old man into shape.

And now I'm trying to talk myself into this being a brilliant turn of events.

In the end, Fie didn't regret reaching out to his family. He hadn't expected his mum to decide a visit was in order and hang up without further conversation, but the next few days would be interesting.

I should've called Dad.

Whistling for Haggard, Fie decided to wander through the village. The walk and fresh air might make him less terrified of the impending visit. He meandered toward the police station to check on Sid. The officer in the front waved him on through, and Jacinda waved him over.

"Hello, Haggard. Have you been a good boy?" Jacinda immediately reached into her desk and tossed a biscuit over. "Such a beautiful dog. I'm supposed to be enjoying myself, but no, I've gotten called in on my day off. Sid was in his office with his father. They didn't shout at each other, so that's good. His father left a few minutes ago."

"Do I get a hello?" Fie asked.

Jacinda grabbed a second dog treat to hold out to him. "Want a biscuit?"

Fie chuckled when Haggard immediately shifted forward to sit in front of her. "He can have it on my behalf."

"Go on. He's been hiding in there since his dad left." Jacinda gave Haggard's ear a scratch. "He can relax out here with me if you like."

"Just don't feed him too many biscuits." Fie headed over to Sid's office with Haggard huffing at him. *Too bloody smart for his own good.* He opened the door to find Sid face down on his desk. "Having a good day?"

"Brilliantly shit."

"My family is coming to visit."

Sid sat up slowly with a grin spreading across his face. "Are they? All of them?"

"No idea." Fie leaned over to steal a few cold chips from the open container on the desk. "Maybe. Prepare yourself to have your cheeks pinched."

"Which ones?"

"You never know with my family." Fie made a note to give his dad a call about the visit. Davet wouldn't handle being pounced on by a pack of enthusiastic Scots. "My mum got a little excited when I called."

"I invited my dad to dinner with us." Sid offered his own good news.

"Us?"

"You and Davet."

Fie grabbed a handful of chips. "Well, if he's not

scarred for life by your father, my family will finish the job beautifully."

"I'd hoped for more than one night." Sid scrubbed his face vigorously with his fingers.

"Heard about Mrs Knight. You all right?"

"Oh, brilliant, so all right I invited my old man to dinner with my two male lovers. What could possibly go wrong?" Sid dropped his head against the desk again with a painful-sounding thud. "We're fucked."

"Cheer up."

Sid tilted his head to the side to look at Fie. "Oh?"

"My mum will bring cake." Fie knew they had issues to deal with. All of them, with their families. "So we'll have awkward conversation and cake."

"With a side of bigoted arsehole?" Sid groaned.

"He might behave himself." Fie hoped Sid's father was serious about reconciliation. It would be cruel to yank his son around with the potential of having family in his life again. "If he doesn't, my mum will go after him with her rolling pin."

"Kept thinking about Mrs Knight dying alone in her little cottage with her tiny dog. Her children rarely came to visit," Sid admitted. "How long had she been on the floor with no one bothering to see her? What if my dad dies as well? I'll be the one getting a call from a police detective. He's got no one but me. When was the last time I spoke to him outside of this past month?"

"Mrs Knight was a lovely woman who had a kind word for everyone." Fie understood the fear, though

Sid had perhaps forgotten the truth in the face of his guilt. "Your father disowned you. He didn't want you around."

From the half-hearted shrug, Sid clearly didn't believe him. Fie decided to let it go. Some demons had to be fought on their own; he could only be there to help, not fix the issue for Sid.

"Can you sneak out early?"

"From a police station?" Sid cracked a barely there smile at his own joke. "My shift is already over. I'm only putting off my report on Mrs Knight. Struggling to find words. Whatever I write will be official and professional, not a representation of who she was."

"You can't save everyone, Sid. Her dying alone isn't your fault. Writing your report doesn't make you a bad person." Fie decided not to consider the irony of his words, telling himself this situation was nothing like the survivor's guilt he felt.

We're all messed up, aren't we?

"I've always wanted to fuck on this desk."

"First, sex isn't an answer to your problems." Fie glowered sternly at him. "Second, you can't be quiet even when you try. I'd rather not have Jacinda hear you shouting out my name mid-coitus. She'd never let us hear the end of it."

"Spoilsport."

CHAPTER THIRTY

DAVET

I should've said no.

Davet eyed his reflection critically in the full-length mirror in his bedroom. He grabbed his phone to text a photo to Simone with a simple question, *Can I meet Sid's dad in this?*

Is there an etiquette to meeting one of your lovers' family for the first time?

Both Fox and Rabbit remained unmoved by his current crisis. They lay curled up together on the comfortable armchair he'd gotten from his uncle. His aunt had been the one to explain that the furniture translated into Santos's version of an apology.

They had talked, but not much. Davet tried not to take the distance between them personally. Santos had to figure out how to be both a brother and an uncle.

Returning his thoughts to Sid's dysfunctional family and away from his own, Davet grabbed a shirt from his bed to hold in front of him. *Too wrinkled. Hate ironing. No.* He wanted to be comfortable, yet dressed up enough to make a good impression.

When am I ever capable of being comfortable meeting a stranger? Never. This is going to be a nightmare.

Davet dug underneath a shirt to find his phone when it rang. "Why do you call me when I text you? Aren't you supposed to message me with a reply?"

"I'll make it quick," Simone promised. "I don't have the energy to mess around typing with my fingers. Wear your dark jeans and the vintage T-shirt I sent you from my trip to Milan, and wear your comfort hoodie. If they plan to fob a family supper on you this soon, they can accept you as is. Oh, and brush your hair."

"I always—"

"Must go. Text me after." Simone was gone before he had a chance to finish his sentence.

Typical.

With his outfit decided, Davet spent almost an hour showering. He shampooed his hair twice after forgetting mid-conditioner if he'd washed it first. Stress always made him obsess over every detail within his control.

What if Sid's dad hates me so much I ruin their reconciliation? I don't know how to talk to him. I haven't practised any possible conversations yet. What if I lose my words or panic and say the wrong thing? I can't do this.

Breathe.

Yes, I can.

I can do this.

It's only supper with Fie and Sid plus one extra person.

I'll be fine.

By late in the afternoon, Davet had gone over twenty potential conversations with himself. The topics might not come up, but practising lowered his stress. He also envisioned worst-case scenarios and how to talk his way out of them.

Sid had suggested one of the quieter restaurants in Bideford. Davet hated the added anxiety of going out put on an already stressful situation. He did see the point of Mr Little being less inclined to verbally explode in a public environment; then again, his parents had never been bothered about an audience when causing a scene.

His anxiety continued to build until Davet left an hour early for Fie's cottage just to keep from reorganising his Coffee First kitchen for the third time. They planned to go to the restaurant together to present a united front. He wasn't completely sure what Sid meant by that.

United front sounded like an insurance company to him.

Fox and Rabbit had been fed and watered. Davet left them in their room. He didn't want to risk either running—or hopping—wild at Fie's or the restaurant.

Carrying his hoodie, Davet walked across the field

and up the lane toward Fie's, his mind considering all the ways the evening might go wrong. He hated the unknown aspect of Mr Little.

"Hello, Haggard." Davet greeted Fie's dog, who'd raced out to meet him. He followed him toward the back door. "Have you escaped?"

"Davet." Sid waved him inside, spotting him through the kitchen window. "Swayze's taking a quick shower. How'd all your coffee go this morning?"

"Hot, mostly. The coffee I mean." Davet blinked in surprise when Sid grabbed his wrist to drag him closer. He wound up squashed between the refrigerator and Sid's body. This had not been a part of the evening he'd practised. "Hello."

"Oh, we can manage a better hello than that, can't we?" Sid brought his hand up to slide underneath Davet's shirt, his fingers splaying along Davet's side. "You okay with a kiss?"

"Just one?" He caught Sid by his shirt and closed the short distance between their lips. "How much of a greeting is that? Shouldn't we be thorough?"

Long, lazy kisses made for quite a welcome. Davet's anxiety quickly faded away. Another, slightly harder, issue appeared in the lower half of his body.

How am I supposed to deal with an erection before supper?

"Did you have to start without me?" Fie stood in the hallway with a towel around his waist, drops of water clinging to the hair on his chest. He made an enticing picture in the late afternoon sun filtering in through the window. "Why don't you two help me dry off?"

CHAPTER THIRTY-ONE

Sid

A naked, wet Fie along with Davet pressed against his body, gave Sid no doubts they weren't going to be leaving for the restaurant on time. They had a more important issue to deal with first: his hard cock. A little sexual healing would do wonders for the day he'd suffered through.

He and Fie had turned to focus on Davet, who'd immediately pulled away. He'd apparently had an intense day and needed to avoid sensory overload. Sid didn't pretend to understand; he wanted this to work, so learning to adjust for Davet wasn't a hardship.

Checking the clock on the wall, Sid realised they had a limited opportunity for fun. He dropped to his knees in front of Fie, yanking his towel off and flinging the fabric behind him. Fie's cock twitched when he blew across the head.

Sid glanced over his shoulder to see Davet stroking

himself through his jeans. Davet stumbled backwards slightly and sat heavily in a chair. "Enjoy the show."

He wanted to take this slowly, but Fie had other plans. They wound up stretched out on the kitchen rug head to cock, not far from Davet, who appeared unable to look away from them. Haggard had run off to hide in the other room.

His fingers toyed with Fie's balls while his tongue teased the head of his shaft. Focusing became difficult with Fie returning the favour—and then some. Quiet moans from Davet only served to add an additional layer to the growing heat in the room.

Having stripped out of his jeans, Davet had pulled a condom out of his wallet to cover his shaft. Sid didn't judge him for the slightly unusual requirement. They all had their preferences.

If condoms allowed him to enjoy sex without stress, who cared? They'd also discovered he enjoyed watching Sid and Fie together. A new kink he'd apparently not known about himself: he was a voyeur in the making.

Shifting on his side slightly, Sid managed to keep an eye on Davet while more enthusiastically beginning to move his mouth on Fie's shaft. He flicked his tongue in the way he knew Fie enjoyed the most. His hips bucked up against Sid almost immediately.

Knowing slow wasn't an option, Sid went from teasing to aggressively pushing Fie toward completion. Their competitive sides kicked in, turning their kitchen sixty-nine into a race for who could make the other come first. *And we're both winners.*

Sid lost himself in the growing pleasure of giving and receiving. He barely heard Fie's shout of warning before he won the race. They both did, with Davet following not long after, almost sliding out of his chair. "I can't move."

"You'll have to get up." Davet recovered first, discarding his condom quickly in the rubbish bin and washing his hands multiple times. "You two need to get dressed."

"Can't move." Sid eventually untangled himself from Fie with a groan. "You need a better carpet in the kitchen, Swayze. Not only do I have rug burn, but the floor put my back out."

"We're going to be late." Davet didn't seem able to maintain his relaxed state. He kept checking his watch. "We need to leave soon; even driving might not get us there on time."

With military precision, Sid and Fie cleaned themselves up and got dressed—again. Davet fidgeted in the kitchen waiting for them. He seemed increasingly panicked by watching the clock.

The three men drove across the village far too fast with a police detective behind the wheel. Sid winced when they arrived to find his father had been seated for over ten minutes. *Fuck. We're off to a rocky start, and we haven't even gotten around to ordering drinks yet.*

"I'm Davet Heuse, Mr Little. Sid's told me so much

about you." Davet broke the silence and held his hand out while studiously avoiding the stern gaze being directed at him. "I'm sorry we kept you waiting."

With three sentences and a handshake, Davet seemed to run out of his practised greeting. Sid stepped in and completed the introductions—or reintroduction, in Fie's case. His father had gone into a bit of shock by the two additions to their supper, likely more by the implication than their physical presence in the restaurant.

Sid sat across from his father with Fie and Davet on either side of the square table. Haggard stretched himself out underneath by Fie's feet, a snoring distraction. "Have you ordered yet?"

"No. I prefer being polite and waiting for everyone to arrive." His father glowered at him.

"Right." Sid shifted in his chair, feeling like a child about to be punished for being naughty. "Their shepherd's pie is brilliant."

Groaning internally, Sid considered calling the façade of a family supper off. They'd doomed the evening from the start by arriving late, even though only by ten minutes. He wondered if they should even waste energy on eating.

"You're gay." His father didn't wait for drinks or breadsticks to fire his question at Fie. "You."

"I'm not," Davet offered, stepping into the conversation before Fie could respond. "Bisexual. I'm sexually ambidextrous."

Sid snickered at the joke, ignoring his father's glare. "Sexually ambidextrous."

"How old are you?" His father seemed so out of his element that Sid wondered if he regretted trying to reach a compromise with him. "Both of you. All three together. Is it legal?"

"Yes." Sid wanted to drown himself in the sea at that moment. He'd never brought a date home to meet his parents, for obvious reasons. Only a few minutes into supper confirmed all of his old fears. "Legal. Maybe not socially accepted by everyone, but I've never given two shits about mass acceptance."

"As it—"

Davet surprised Sid by hitting the table with his fist and leaning forward to interrupt. "You have a chance with your son. Do you have enough life left to risk throwing away an opportunity to find common ground together?"

"Why don't we all start the evening over?" Fie broke the awkward silence that followed Davet's outburst. "We've placed so much pressure on this that none of us are relaxed. Let's take a deep breath, order our meal, and attempt to simply have a nice supper."

After pointing to an item on the menu in Sid's hand, Davet bolted out of the restaurant. The three men left behind stared at his retreating form. Sid asked Fie to order for both of them then went outside himself.

He stepped through the front door to find Davet standing there, berating himself. With Fie dealing with his father, he turned his attention to calming the anxious autistic. He was proud of Davet for being able to get his thoughts across when sometimes he struggled with words himself in tense situations.

"Are you all right?" Sid asked when Davet stopped ranting in French. "I'm not upset, by the way. You said what I'd been thinking. And honestly, I'd have been far ruder than you were."

I'd have told the stubborn arse to sod off out the door, which wouldn't help anything.

"All my practice went out the window." Davet tugged on his hoodie despite the balmy evening. He shoved his hands into the pockets. "Telling him off was not on my list of conversation topics. I'm so sorry."

"Don't be." Sid leaned against the back of a bench outside of the restaurant. "I'm glad you said what you did. You more than Fie can understand toxic family issues."

Davet shrugged, continuing to walk a small circuit following a crack in the pavement. "Not my place to get involved."

Ahh, yes, is it too early for this conversation?
I am so not equipped.
Fuck.
Don't bugger this up, Sidney.

"A few dates and sex might not seem like enough for a deep connection to develop. We've known each other for years now, and Fie and I both want you in our lives. Not for a short time, either. You matter to us.

Your thoughts, opinions, all of you." Sid floundered to find the right words to express his developing feelings. None of them were quite ready for that. "You've a place with us."

Davet didn't seem to know how to respond. "I—"

"Are you Fraco's brother?" One of the restaurant's waiters came over, interrupting Davet mid-sentence while puffing on his vape.

"He is." Sid narrowed his gaze on the young man. "Detective Inspector Little. Can we help you?"

"How about not glaring at me like my nan and I'll help you? I'm Alan." He didn't hold his hand out, which was good because Sid was struggling to not knock the vape out of his mouth.

Youth these days.

Oh, fuck me, I'm turning into my father.

"How can you help me?" Sid asked. He restrained his own innate sarcasm to give him the benefit of the doubt.

"I went to college with Fraco and his roomies." Alan jogged away to set his e-cigarette on a brick wall after Davet started sneezing. "Fraco hated the smell as well. We had a few courses together. He was a lovely bloke who never drank even once. In fact, he never went to the pub with us."

"And?" Sid kept his eye on Davet, who kept playing with the zipper on his hoodie. "Did you have information for us?"

"I'd have said something earlier but...." Alan

hesitated, then lifted his hands when Sid's glower deepened. "I honestly wasn't sure I knew anything at all. They switched universities, moved away, and that's a bit odd, right?"

Sid wanted to shake the young man to get him to spit out whatever information he clearly had. Years of police investigation and military service allowed him to easily rein in his impatience. "Quite odd, yes."

Alan glanced over at Davet then back at Sid. "They liked a prank. Fraco made an easy target since half the time he never realised they'd even played one. They got him drunk once, and Fraco thought his supper had gone off."

Sid breathed through the sudden rage that filled him. "And you never thought to mention that to anyone? Either before or after his death?"

"Just a joke, wasn't it? Harmless prank." He shrugged. "I don't know for certain they ever got him drunk again."

"He died. Not so much a prank as potentially voluntary manslaughter." Sid placed a hand on Davet's shoulder when he swayed on his feet. "You'll be all right, Davet. I promise."

"A harmless prank? Always fun to pick at someone who can't understand," Davet hissed at the young waiter. "Disgusting."

Sid stepped back when Davet stormed into the restaurant. He waited for the door to shut then scowled once again at Alan. "I want you at the station in the morning, eight o'clock sharp. You'll give me a full statement on what you can remember about these pranks and the days around Fraco's death. Are we clear?"

"Yes, sir."

"If you're not, I'll be having a word with your nan." Sid knew Alan's family. His grandmother could strike fear into anyone. "Bloody harmless pranks."

Without another word, Alan disappeared around the corner with his vape. Sid hoped he didn't have to chase him down for questioning. They might finally be able to get answers on Fraco's death.

After calming himself down, Sid returned to the restaurant. Everyone at the table had gone eerily quiet. He wondered if they'd all wind up with indigestion from all the anxiety.

"I'm sorry."

"What?" Sid stared in surprise at his father, who'd been quite intent on his duck with potatoes and cabbage.

"Whatever my thoughts on your relationship, you're my son. I do love you." His father set his fork to the side. "I'm sorry."

Sid had three men intently staring at him waiting for a response, though to be fair, Davet's gaze was focused on his nose. "I accept your apology."

Most sodding awkward apology and acceptance in the history of humanity.

For God's sake.

"Do you hug now?" Davet asked. "Don't normal

people hug after making up with one another?"

"You are normal." Sid rolled his eyes. He didn't feel very touchy-feely at the moment.

"So, no hug?" he asked seriously.

Christmas dinner is going to be a fucking nightmare with our families combined.

CHAPTER THIRTY-TWO

DAVET

Curiosity had kept Davet up most of the night. He served coffee to his early birds then closed up with a sticker on the front shop window about a family emergency. If Sid found out anything at all about Fraco's death, he wanted to be on hand to hear immediately.

Was Alan's insinuation from the night before right? Had Fraco in essence been pranked to death? Davet had to know the truth, no matter how painful.

With a box filled with coffees for the detectives, Davet carefully made his way to see Sid. The hot drinks disappeared in seconds upon his arrival. They descended on him like they'd walked through the Sahara for one drop of liquid, and he held the only water left in the world.

One of the detectives paused in chugging his coffee to explain Sid hadn't finished questioning a witness. Davet sat in a hallway outside Sid's office, watching the hustle and bustle of the police work around him. He wanted his answer and had no issues patiently waiting all day if necessary.

"Davet!" Jacinda greeted him with her usual enthusiasm thirty minutes later. She dropped into the chair beside him. "Sid's almost done. Our sergeant wants a word with him first, but he shouldn't be long."

"Fraco's case?" Davet knew she'd likely try to couch her words for his sake but he pushed on for answers regardless. "Did Alan have anything useful to say about my brother's death?"

Jacinda started to shake her head before he finished his query. "Sid will explain what he can. I don't know all the details."

Davet frowned at her; she was definitely holding something back. "Fine."

"Someone brought a ginger cake in this morning. Want a slice?"

"*No.*" He winced at the sharpness in his voice. "Thank you."

Oh yes, the thank-you will definitely negate my practically shouting at her.

Don't be rude to the detectives. They mean well.

Everybody means well.

They mean well right up to not actually helping me.

After a few more minutes of uncomfortable small talk, Jacinda took the hint and left him to his thoughts. Davet slouched in the hard chair. He stared up at the ceiling, counting all the spots on the tiles.

Another thirty minutes went by before Sid finally made an appearance. He smiled when Davet sat up and waved. They headed into his office, and Sid closed the door behind them.

Sid dragged him into the corner of the office where no one could see them through the windows, and captured Davet's lips in a quick and hungry kiss. "Morning. Have a seat."

"We've gone past morning."

Sid glanced at his watch. "Not quite, but almost. Sit, sit."

The forced upbeat energy worried Davet. His anxiety notched up several levels. What exactly had Alan told Sid?

Davet shifted over to stand by the chair. His body didn't quite get the message to sit down. "Just tell me? Please?"

"I spoke with Alan earlier. He brought along one of Fraco's roommates as well." Sid eased into his chair with a sense of uneasiness that even Davet could pick up on. "They did trick Fraco into drinking that night, and then went out for a bit of fun by the canal with more alcohol. None of them remember at what point Fraco wandered off. He, according to their statement, walked away unnoticed. They claimed to have never wanted him hurt."

"Only humiliated and sick? Their personal, favourite joke. An easy target." Davet clenched his fists tightly, restraining the urge to punch a wall.

"Do you believe them?"

"Mostly." Sid stood and moved around his desk toward Davet. "My years of experience tell me they likely saw him after he went into the water. I believe they tried to save him, failed, and ran out of fear of being found out."

"He died alone." Davet struggled to breathe through the oppressive weight suddenly pressing on his chest with a vengeance. "Confused and afraid in the cold."

"I know." Sid stepped in front of him with his arms open. Davet appreciated him waiting to see if a hug was actually wanted, not just forcing it on him. "So, I spoke with Fie before I came to see you, told him what we learned. We want to take a trip down to the beach, not Pennecombe as it'll be packed about now. There's the more private one not far from it. Why don't we celebrate Fraco's life together? The three of us. You don't have to be alone. Let us be there for you."

Davet hesitantly leant forward until his head rested against Sid's chest. "I'm angry."

"You've every right to be." Sid raised his arm to wrap around Davet. "Answers don't make it better, but now you know the truth. My Detective Chief Inspector's decided against pursuing them. She believes the court will find it accidental. I'm sorry."

What does it matter?

Fraco isn't coming back.

He didn't feel any better for knowing. Maybe with distance, he might. For now, it was a struggle not to chase down Fraco's roommates and vent his anger on them.

Sid held him until Davet managed to breathe normally. "C'mon. Let's escape before my DCI decides I've another report to write."

Their beach excursion hadn't been timed perfectly. The three men arrived as the summer skies opened. Soft rain pelted down, but Davet didn't mind at all.

Sid and Fie followed him down to the shoreline. They huddled together on a large rock on the beach. Davet was squashed between them with their arms wound around his back.

I am not alone.
Not in love, maybe, I don't think, but not alone.
What does love feel like anyway?

Love had always been an abstract concept to Davet. He was fairly certain he'd experienced at least one form of it. Strong emotions always confused him.

Lost in his thoughts, Davet barely noticed when the rain stopped. Sid and Fie eventually led him away, taking him home to dry off. He wasn't even sure goodbyes had been exchanged.

His dazed mood lasted into the evening. Thoughts of love, his brother, family swirled around in his mind. He eventually wandered over to knock on his uncle and aunt's door, needing a connection of some sort.

"Davet?" Santos reached out for him only to stop at his expression. "One of the detectives called us with an update on Fraco's case. I planned to visit you later. Do you want to come inside?"

"You hurt us," Davet insisted. "Fraco and I. But you always cared, I think."

"Of course, I'm your uncle. I love you." Santos pulled Davet into a warm embrace. "I am sorry, son. So incredibly sorry for not doing better. You were right. The adults in your life all failed to some degree, including me."

"I forgive you." Davet shifted out of his uncle's arms. He'd lost enough family and throwing away his relationship with Santos seemed a foolish waste. "Fraco would've forgiven you as well. Catholics do that."

CHAPTER THIRTY-THREE

Fie

Two days after their journey to the beach, Fie was still sweeping up sand. Haggard had made a point to roll around after getting wet. He made a mental note to rinse his dog off before coming into the cottage next time.

"You're enjoying this." He glared at Haggard, who flopped over on his side with his tongue lolling out. "A bath might knock the grin off your face."

Haggard growled at him.

"Would you rather my mum do it? She'll have you sparkling clean in no time."

Haggard stopped growling.

"That's what I thought."

One of his cousins had called to warn him the family convoy had left Scotland. Fie had a few days of respite, given the meandering path his parents usually drove to allow them to see the sights. He'd made a cleaning list in preparation of the Russell invasion.

The bell rang, and Fie paused in the middle of picking up the slight mess in his living room. As Sid and Davet spent more time in his cottage, their stuff had migrated over as well. He'd found fox and rabbit fur while picking up after Haggard.

Santos stood on the other side of the door.

"Are you serious about my nephew?"

Fie had intended to invite the man in but changed his mind at the question. "I could ask you that. Didn't the two of you reconcile the other day?"

"Our Davet had a crush on you and Sid from the day he met you both. He's already halfway in love with you two without realising it." Santos wilted slightly when Fie straightened to his full height, but he didn't back down. "Are you serious about him?"

"Yes."

When Fie refused to say anything further on the subject, Santos eventually left. He wouldn't be baited into an argument with the man. Why bother? Neither of their opinions would be changed in the effort.

Alone again, Fie finished most of the cleaning on his list. Haggard interrupted him late in the afternoon. He'd gone past lunch, forgetting to eat; his stomach grumbled almost as much as Haggard.

"Fancy bacon?" Fie glanced down at Haggard, who wagged his tail.

I'm a few more grey hairs away from being a grumpy hermit who only talks to his dog.

He got bread and bacon out for a sandwich only to put them both away seconds later. *I don't have to eat on my own, hiding away in my cottage.* Decision made, he sent two quick text messages and then left with Haggard trotting along beside him.

The rain had cooled off the stark heat of summer. Fie enjoyed the breeze off the sea and the bit of sunlight peeking through the clouds. The salty air made him breathe in deeply and release some of the stress he'd held on to.

"Fie." Davet waved from where he sat in the middle of the field not far from his cottage and shop. Rabbit and Fox were napping together next to him. "Uncle Santos went storming by earlier. What did you say?"

"Nothing," Fie answered honestly. He crouched in front of Davet, keeping an eye on the three animals. "Sid should finish work in about ten minutes. How about I pick up fish and chips for us all and come back?"

"A picnic?"

"A greasy one." Fie smiled when Davet patted him on the knee briefly. He'd grown more comfortable with them over time. "Want something else?"

Davet shook his head and returned to reading his book. "No vinegar."

"I know, we're uncivilised with our malt vinegar and overly greasy chips." Fie almost fell backwards when Davet shifted forward to kiss him. "Well, hello."

Instead of responding, Davet hid behind his novel.

Fie knew about the little club he and Shirley had created for reading. He left Davet to his book and continued on his way, not surprised when Haggard rather unwillingly followed.

Haggard had grown attached to Davet, or more accurately, to Fox and Rabbit. The three animals had defied his expectations and not tried to eat one another. He'd honestly believed the bunny would've been at least slightly nibbled.

If I believed in ghosts, I'd say Fraco stayed around to keep his animals happy.

Fie would've left Haggard with his furry friends, but he felt naked without his service animal. He'd healed leaps and bounds, particularly in the last six months—more than all the years before—yet part of him remained bruised.

Maybe a sliver of his heart would always be shattered.

Packets of fish and chips in hand, Fie returned to find Davet being smothered by a familiar Scottish horde with an amused Sid hovering on the edge. His cousin had obviously lied about how soon his family would arrive. He reached into the chattering group to extract Davet, who looked beyond overwhelmed.

"Morogh." Fie's father stood impossibly taller and broader than Fie, while his mother appeared as tiny as ever. They converged on him to crush him into a hug that reminded him of home and a time when his heart hadn't been scarred beyond repair. Tears sprang instantly to his eyes. "Are you finished keeping us away, lad? I've missed you."

His shirt grew damp from where his mother had clearly begun to weep, hopefully with happy tears. Fie thought he'd outgrown a need for a hug from his parents. His father was content to hold both his wife and son tightly.

"Now, introduce us to your young men." His mother pulled away from them, wiping her eyes with a handkerchief. "Properly."

Fie ignored the snort of amusement from Sid and the other family members. "You've already mobbed both of them. Detective Inspector Sidney Little and Davet Heuse. And the furry buggers are Haggard, Rabbit, and Fox. Don't ask; I didn't name the last two."

"Morogh." His mother sent him a glare that made his three cousins who'd made the journey pretend to fear for his life. "That's enough nonsense. Why don't the lot of you find a takeaway and bring food for all of us? Hmm? We can all enjoy a picnic."

After a little teasing, his cousins and their parents disappeared with Sid and Davet. Fie found himself alone with his parents and the animals. His mother had immediately sat in the grass with the rabbit in her lap and the other two on either side of her.

Sid had gone to the back of Davet's cottage to find a few empty crates to bring over for them to use as makeshift chairs. His mother ignored the one he set in front of her, so he sat beside her as well. "Did you enjoy the drive down?"

She reached over to grasp his hand. "I've never enjoyed a drive less. I spent all of my time wishing we'd already gotten to Devon. We've missed you so very much. Now, tell me about your young men."

"They're not that young. Sid's almost my age." Fie reminded himself he was in his forties and well beyond blushing over being quizzed on his dating. "You've both met him before."

"Have we?" His father grunted. He sat on one of the crates. "I'm going to break this damned thing. Tell us about them anyway. Are you being safe?"

"Shite."

"Watch your language, love." His mother tutted at him, seeming more amused than upset. They'd always enjoyed winding Fie up even in his youth. "Should we buy condoms for you? We've a Costco near us now. I could get them in bulk to save you money."

"You should see the size of the pickle jar. Had a devil of a time getting the lid off the first time." His father pulled his phone out to fumble around with it until he found a photo to hold out to Fie. "Took a picture. It's bigger than my head."

"We're not nattering about those sort of pickles right now."

Fie pinched the bridge of his nose and counted to ten, twenty, and then thirty. He had to laugh at the playful argument his parents were having over pickles—or *pickles*. "I've missed you two. So very much."

"Well, you've done a funny job of showing it." His father didn't pull any punches. "Have you tried the Costco pickles?"

"*Darach*," his mother snapped exasperatedly. "I regret buying the stinky things."

"No appreciation for the finer foods in life."

Fie exchanged a grimace with his mother. "I appreciate them being far away from me."

CHAPTER THIRTY-FOUR

SID

Sid and Davet followed the four large Scottish men and Fie's aunt, a brown-haired woman who stood at barely five foot but managed to lead her sons and husband around with a snap of her fingers. They chattered amongst themselves like oversized, bearded squirrels. Davet seemed almost entranced by them.

What Sid loved most about the Russell clan was how they reminded him of Fie before Afghanistan. The man who'd joked and laughed as much if not more than himself. He relished the boisterous laughter that swirled around the group.

Sid belatedly remembered Davet might not appreciate the sheer volume of the Russells. He eased closer to wrap an arm around his shoulders. "Why don't we sneak over to Shirley's to get one of those quiches you like? Fie's fish and chips will be cold by the time we get this lot organised and back to your cottage."

"Are you sure Fie's related to them? He's quiet as a mouse in comparison to his cousins." Davet didn't comment when Sid changed directions toward the bakery across from the fish and chip shop. "She hugged me. Fie's mum. It was nice. I think. Weird, nice."

"The mum hug was mostly nice, then?" Sid had been about to rescue Davet earlier when Fie returned. Mum Russell had a way of sweeping everyone into her embrace. "They definitely take getting used to. The entire lot of them."

"Is Fie adopted?" Davet seemed genuinely confused by the stark contrast between the Russells and their lost lamb. "Or, no, he can't be. He looks exactly like his father."

Sid held onto his laughter by the skin of his teeth. Davet might misunderstand and think he was being laughed at. "He used to act like his cousins."

Davet shook his head in disbelief. "Fie? He laughs, sure, but not like his cousins."

"Trauma changes you." Sid had often wondered if Fie hadn't returned a completely different man. "He and I used to be identical personality-wise, before we went off to war. He never fully regained himself."

"You seem unchanged," Davet asked. His statement came out as more of a question. "Your friend Jane claims you don't let things affect you. She said it's weird, but my emotions don't show on my face much, and people call me strange. I didn't want to argue with her, though. She's a bit scary."

"She is. It's more Fie internalised a lot of his pain and withdrew from everyone. I tried to release mine and heal." Sid had exorcised his demons early after coming home. He'd refused to bury all of it inside. "He's getting better."

"Davet! And your copper." Shirley greeted them with a wave of flour-covered hands, which she brushed off on her doughnut-print pinafore. "You never mentioned stopping by today. What are you hungry for? I've a roasted tomato, basil, and parmesan quiche fresh out of the oven. Does that tempt your tummies at all?"

Sid saw Davet's mood brighten almost instantly. "Sold. How much for the whole pie? Mum Russell will want to try some. Oh, Shirl, you've made those chocolate parcels again. All of those as well. Maybe not all. I wouldn't want to be greedy. Ten quid says Jacinda will be by later to have some as well."

Part of the magic of Shirley's bakery had been her taking standard pastry parcels and turning them into magical sweet treats. Sid had several favourites, including her Black Forest one. He'd never tasted anything better.

By the time the Russells checked in on them, Sid had eaten two and a half chocolate pastries, bought an additional ten plus the quiche, and sent a box of biscuits to the police station for the night shift. Shirley promised to deliver them when she closed up shop for the evening. She'd chatted with Davet about their novel while Sid ate the flaky, sweet deliciousness.

The journey back to the cottage went far more quickly. Hungry stomachs made the Russell cousins less likely to poke and prod at one another. Their mother kept them from eating along the journey.

When they arrived at Davet's cottage, Fie and his parents were deep in conversation. Sid thought he seemed lighter. Time with family had worked wonders for him already.

The Russells had rented a cottage near the sea, one large enough to house all of them. Sid wondered if the place would still be standing when they returned to Scotland. He hoped the owner had insurance.

"Hear you're cosied up with our little Fie." Fie's uncle Glenn came to perch on a crate next to Sid. "You and the coffeemonger here."

Sid opted not to point out Fie was broader shouldered than both he and Davet. He didn't know if Glenn thought positively or negatively about a relationship between three men. "We are. Your *little* nephew has been quite happy with us."

Glenn grinned broadly at him. "Never liked his ex-boyfriend, Edmund. Too driven by making money, that one. You two should do the job nicely. Break his heart, and I'll feed your bollocks to my sheep."

Davet leant closer to Sid when Glenn wandered off. "I believe he's related to Fie."

"Don't worry. I'll protect your bollocks." Sid lowered his voice when Fie's mother came over to sit where her brother-in-law had been. "Mum Russell."

"Sidney." She shifted the crate even closer to them. She placed a hand on Sid's and one on Davet's. "You're both welcome to come visit us anytime, you know. I'm pleased my Morogh's found someone to trust his heart with. You'll be kind to one another, or I'll bash your skulls together until you're all sorted. Now, where'd you hide those chocolate pastries?"

Sid pulled the paper bag hidden behind him. "Davet—"

"Oh yes. Your lovely Fox and Rabbit kept me company." She twisted on the crate to face Davet. "Now, Morogh said you're autistic. You tell us if we're too much. I won't have my circus of a family making life harder for you when they all know how to use their inside voices. Is your shop doing well?"

Davet nodded.

She patted his hand gently then released him. "You're a lovely man. If these blockheads don't treat you well, come up to visit us. We'll fix you right up with the sexy bartender who lives near our farm."

Davet glanced over at her then at Sid, not quite meeting their gazes. "Thank you?" He got up to hug Fie's mother, then darted into his cottage with his two animals.

Sid watched him go. "He needs a minute to settle himself."

"We're a lot for someone who appreciates quiet." She pierced Sid with her sharp gaze. "Thank you."

"Pardon?"

"Thank you." She clutched his hand in both of hers. "You upended your life to keep an eye on our Morogh. You'd no other reason to move to Devon at all. How long have you loved my son?"

"I…." Sid froze in his seat. He didn't want to admit the one secret kept buried deep inside. He'd loved Fie for ages, and somehow Davet had wormed his way into his heart as well. "Years. A painfully long time."

"Tell them," she said knowingly. "Both of them."

"It's too soon." He didn't want to scare them off, particularly Davet. "We've only been on a few dates."

"And known each other for a while? It's never too soon for an 'I love you', Sidney." She squeezed his hand then slowly got to her feet. "I'll collect my circus and lead them off to our rented cottage for a rest. Why don't you three enjoy your evening together? Use condoms."

Sid fell off his crate, landing on the leftover quiche. He grimaced at the mess now squished into his trousers. "Sod it."

Fie helped him to his feet, and they watched his family head off. "You've a roasted tomato on your arse."

"Eat it."

"The tomato or your arse?"

"Both." Sid glanced back at his trousers with a grimace. "Will anyone notice if I drive around in my boxers?"

Cleaning up the mess, they decided to check on

Davet in his cottage. They found him in his bedroom with headphones. He waved them inside when Sid poked his head into the room.

"Why are you holding a towel to your trousers?" Davet pulled out his headphones and tried to peer around Sid. "Did you sit on something?"

"He sat on your quiche."

Sid glared at Fie. "I fell over."

"On the quiche."

The innocent teasing quickly devolved. Sid stripped out of his trousers and boxers, the latter definitely unnecessary. Fie had them lined up on the edge of the rather small bed with Davet squeezed in the middle. They traded kisses while stroking each other's cocks.

"Suck him." Fie grabbed Sid's head and pressed him toward Davet's groin. His other hand went to Davet to guide him down to Fie's shaft. "Oh, yes."

With Fie's hand controlling the movements of his head, Sid focused on Davet's cock and stroking his own. He barely heard Fie's heaving breathing over the sound of his own. The bed creaked, but they all ignored it.

He was so focused on the cock in his mouth, Sid complained when Fie lifted his head off. He grabbed Davet and shifted his body to stretch between them. Sid fumbled around to grab the condoms and lube from the nightstand beside the bed.

Sid almost fell backwards when Davet swallowed his cock whole. His eyes closed to enjoy the warm mouth, oblivious to everything else going on in the room. *"Fuck."*

His ability to focus evaporated completely. He opened his eyes to watch in a haze while Fie slid slowly into Davet from behind. Fie's hand held up Davet's leg while he stroked his own condom-covered cock.

With each thrust of Fie's hips, the bed creaked even further. Davet stroked himself in time while sucking hard on Sid's cock. Sid stroked his fingers along both of their bodies, pinching nipples and tugging on their hair, even tracing around the lips stretched around his shaft.

Taking one of the condoms, Sid eased Davet up to roll one on his cock. He didn't want to ruin the moment by triggering Davet's sensitivity issues. They settled for stroking each other while Fie continued rocking up into him.

Fie pressed Davet's head toward Sid; the two kissed while he watched. They'd discovered Davet tended to get easily distracted by speaking during sex. Sid found it difficult at times, but he didn't mind the compromise, particularly considering how close to the edge those skilful fingers on his shaft had brought him.

Between the kissing and the stroking, Sid didn't last long. He was able to turn his attention to Davet fully. His greatest pleasure actually came from watching Davet and Fie lose control over themselves.

Cries of enjoyment were quickly followed by a massive crack and them sliding into one another when the bed collapsed. Sid roared with laughter while Fie attempted to extract Davet from between them. He'd gotten crushed under their larger bodies.

"You broke my bed." Davet stood, staring down at the damaged frame. "Oh, it's sticky."

Pressing his lips down to stop his laughter, Sid helped Davet get the condom off his leg. He immediately ran out of the room to the shower. Sid exchanged a glance with Fie before they both snickered at the destruction of the bed.

"It's all those chocolate pastries you gobbled down earlier," Fie teased him.

"*Arse.*"

They cleaned up as much as possible while Davet washed himself off, hopefully stemming a sensory meltdown before it started. Sid tossed their used condoms in the bin and helped Fie attempt to fix the frame. They failed.

"So, sleepover at your place?" Sid got a pillow in the face for his trouble. "What? You've a bigger cottage and bed."

Several hours later, stretched out on Fie's bed, Sid's thoughts returned to his earlier conversation with Mrs Russell. *Love.* Was it too early? He'd known Fie since their twenties and Davet for two years. *When do I say I love you? Is there a perfect time for it?*

CHAPTER THIRTY-FIVE

Davet

Sunlight hitting his face woke Davet up abruptly. He twisted around in confusion. *What happened to my alarm?*

Oh no.

Rubbing the sleep from his eyes, Davet tried to extract himself from between Fie and Sid. Their arms tightened around him. He slipped his hands down along their bodies to wrap around their soft cocks.

He had their full attention after several minutes of sliding his fingers up and down. "Morning. Can you let me up now?"

"Not just yet."

Not just yet turned into an extended period cramped in Fie's shower. Davet tried to rush, but two naked bodies were impossible to resist. He eventually managed to get out of the bathroom, dressed, and jogged all the way to his cottage.

Setting up quickly, Davet managed to open up without any of his regulars waiting more than a few minutes. Shirley handed over the usual basket of fresh-baked pastries and scones while smirking knowingly at him. He ignored her.

"Came by earlier for a coffee and a natter, but didn't see you. Used my key to check on you, found a broken bed." Shirley poured herself a cup and grinned over the rim at him. "Spend the night elsewhere, did you?"

"Shirley."

After teasing him a while longer, Shirley returned to her bakery. Davet filched one of the breakfast pastries, having missed a chance to eat earlier. He settled into his morning routine, only for Simone to bring his day crashing down around him with a single text.

A mutual friend, whose parents still attended the same church as Davet's parents, had reached out. They'd apparently mentioned that the Heuses intended to spend a week in Bideford to, in their words, "see why the police won't prosecute the monsters who killed our son." Simone had immediately wanted to warn him.

Her exact words, *invasion of the arseholes,* hadn't been wrong. Davet wondered how Fie's family would react to meeting his parents. He had no doubt it was a disaster in the making.

The rest of his day flew by in a distracted blur of panic. Simone had no idea when they'd left France. He texted his auntie, who swore neither she nor his uncle had heard from his parents; she also promised they wouldn't be welcome in their home.

A first.

Davet wouldn't hold his breath. He trusted his aunt. Uncle Santos might be another story. *What am I going to do?*

"Davet?"

He poked his head through the window to find the Russell clan gathered outside. He usually didn't have customers so late in the afternoon. "Shall I put coffee on?"

"No." Fie's father had a voice that boomed enough to remind Davet of a story he'd read of a gentle giant. "We've come to collect you."

"You're supposed to be finished by now. We promised our Morogh not to harass you while your shop was open," Mum Russell, as Sid called her, clarified with an exasperated smile at her husband. "Your two men are going to meet us at one of the cafés in town. Would you care to join us?"

Wrapping up his end of day tasks went quickly with the help of Fie's mother and uncle. The rest stayed out of the cottage. Mum Russell insisted they tended to make life harder rather than easier in a kitchen.

His silence stretched while the group walked ten minutes over to the café. Davet hadn't known what to talk about. He'd spent most of his morning chatting with customers and had run out of words for the moment.

To his surprise, none of the Russells tried to force

small talk on him. They chatted amongst themselves, leaving him to his thoughts. Fie's mum did keep her arm looped with his as she spoke with her sister-in-law.

"There you are!"

Davet tripped over a step when he heard a familiar voice shouting from across the street. "No."

His stopping in the middle of the pavement brought their entire procession to a halt. Fie's father moved through the rest of his family to stand on Davet's other side. They all turned to face the couple storming across the street towards them.

"What have you done? You idiot boy." His mother jumped right in with both feet. She didn't bother introducing herself or even noticing the group of mostly large men around him. "What have you said to your uncle Santos? He refused to let us stay with him; he claims we're no longer welcome in the family. You've obviously lied to him again. Always lying. Ungrateful—"

Mum Russell stepped forward, slightly in front of Davet. "Now, you're this lovely lad's parents, aren't you? We've heard quite a bit about you from our Morogh."

"I'm—"

"We're not interested in whatever lies and cruelty you're about to attempt to bury your poor son under," Fie's mum interrupted for a second time. "You're not welcome here. He's not alone. Davet has a family now with us."

"She's saying to bugger off back to France, you absolute wankers." One of Fie's cousins decided to add his two cents, earning a whack on the head from his mother. "What? I'm not wrong."

"Are you going to allow them to speak to us so rudely? You're our son," his father interjected.

Davet had an entire family behind him, all glaring at his parents. He'd never experienced such an overwhelming amount of support when dealing with them. "I am. I know you're here to harass the police about Fraco's death. You've no say in the matter. Let him rest in peace, finally."

Ignoring his parents' spluttered attempt to argue with him, Davet continued towards the café just down the street. The Russells fell in behind him. Fie's mother wrapped an arm around him while her husband kept glowering over his shoulder.

Both Fie and Sid were standing outside waiting for them. They'd obviously watched the scene from a distance. Davet didn't know how to react when the two men took turns giving him a tight hug and deep kiss by way of greeting.

We're apparently no longer keeping our relationship under wraps around the village.

With a bit of jostling, the group managed to push a few tables together to accommodate them. Davet had expected his parents to follow them inside and make a scene. He spied them being led away by Jacinda through the window.

"What?" Sid smiled innocently at him.

Conversation flowed easily after they ordered. Davet had expected to be overwhelmed, but no one pressed him into speaking. Time alone would come later, and he'd need it.

Davet sat between Fie and Sid, his legs pressed against theirs. He jealously guarded his plate of food when it arrived and Sid tried to steal part of his meal. "Is this life now?"

"Barmy family, good food, promise of mind-blowing sex later?" Sid leaned closer to whisper in his ear. "One can only hope."

"Behave." Fie stretched his arm out to steal a handful of chips from Sid's plate. "And it's more than a promise. It's a guarantee."

I like this life.

It's magnificent.

CHAPTER THIRTY-SIX

Sid

Several months of difficult conversations had led to a dreaded supper with his father. Sid had never believed the stubborn old fool would agree to another meal with his son—and his two lovers. And then he had. They'd opted for a restaurant in a village halfway between Bideford and his dad's home.

All week, Sid had suffered from anxiety gnawing in the pit of his belly. He'd pictured a hundred ways for the supper to go off the rails. In the end, he shrugged off the worry as best he could.

Whatever happened, Sid would have Fie and Davet beside him.

"Simone suggests this." Davet came out of Sid's bedroom carrying one of his dressier shirts and trousers. "She says to brush your hair."

"When do I not brush my hair?"

Determined to make the best impression on Sid's

father, Davet had sent his friend videos of Sid and Fie's wardrobes. Sid had been amused while Fie had definitely been more confused than anything else. Simone, they had been informed, was the authority on how to put an outfit together.

What does that even mean?

It apparently meant dressed up. His father would see right through their ploy. *Do I care? It's helping Davet deal with his anxiety.*

They made their way to the restaurant an hour earlier than necessary. Davet had been about to vibrate out of his skin so Sid decided better leave than sit around at home stressing. His father showed up only thirty minutes later appearing as anxious as they were.

None of them spoke. Fie coughed, and nudged Sid a few times. Davet arranged his silverware repeatedly, refusing to glance up.

Well, this is going brilliantly.

How far through supper can we get without a single word exchanged between us aside from a greeting?

The longer the silence stretched, the more Sid itched to break it. He grew uncharacteristically anxious. Davet even tried to start up a conversation about his fox and rabbit only for them to wither into quiet within minutes.

His father, unfortunately, wound up being the one to break the silence. "How does it even work? With three of you? You can't—"

"Enough." Sid slammed his fists against the table,

truly losing his temper for the first time in ages. "I fucking love them—and you can get the hell out of my life if you can't respect and welcome them into our family."

If Sid thought the silence weighed heavily before, it now seemed to be a lead blanket around them. His father refused to meet his gaze, his face had gone completely pale. Fie reached across the table to rest a hand on Sid's arm to offer comfort.

Getting to his feet and throwing his napkin onto the table, Sid strode out of the restaurant, stonily glaring at the whispering diners who stared at him. He'd wanted to avoid making a scene. *Well, done then, Sidney.* His father would likely be even less inclined to soften his stance.

It doesn't matter.

I'll handle this as I've always done, by ignoring him.

"Sid?" Davet slipped out the front door to join him with a bemused Fie casually following behind. He fidgeted in front of Sid for a second. "You love us?"

Sid had mentally considered all the ways to declare his feelings over the last month, shouting out while cursing his father in the middle of a restaurant hadn't been on the top of his list. "I do. Very much so."

"I love you as well." Davet leaned against the closed restaurant door and stared across the street avoiding their gaze. "Both of you, I mean. Not just Sid. I love Fie as well. And Rabbit, Fox, and Haggard, though not the same as you two. I'm going to stop talking now."

Fie, who had always struggled to express emotions, simply wrapped his arms around both of them. "Why don't we eat at my place?"

"Wait."

Sid glanced over his shoulder to find his father pushing the door open. He hoped they weren't about to make another dramatic scene worthy of a reality show. "Yes?"

His father stepped outside and placed a hand on Sid's arm. "We made a bit of a scene in there so we might want to try the place across the street."

"Why?" Sid didn't fancy the indigestion that would come from prolonging their awkward attempt at dinner. "Why bother?"

"Because your mother will haunt the rest of my days if I don't appreciate two people who love my son." His father's fingers trembled on Sid's arm. "Give me a chance to try, please?"

EPILOGUE

One year later
FIE

A year had made a massive difference to Fie in comparison to all the ones before it, but Guy Fawkes Night would probably always be a bad time for him. Last year Davet had bought him noise-cancelling headphones. They'd discovered the headset drowned out fireworks brilliantly; he'd spent the evening trying to teach Sid and Davet how to make mugs.

It was far less romantic than the movies made out.

Three hours of cleaning, *three*, to get the mess out of their hair. Davet's had been especially difficult. He'd found a dried clay cock stuck under his workbench a few days afterwards, Sid's idea of a joke.

With a little help, Fie had paid him back in kind. He covered Sid's office at the police station with small ceramic cocks. Jacinda had taken great pleasure in setting up a GoPro to record his reaction, after getting permission from the DCI.

"Are you ready?" Davet pulled Fie out of his thoughts.

"Almost." Fie had dreaded today for the past few weeks. He'd allowed Sid to talk him into a military family reunion of sorts on the anniversary of the explosion that had changed all of their lives. "Have they begun to arrive?"

Davet shrugged.

Fie paused in buttoning up his shirt to glance over at Davet fidgeting by the door. "You're nervous."

Davet shrugged again.

The impending invasion had stressed Davet out. He'd only met Jane thus far, and she was the calmest out of the bunch.

"You'll be fine." Fie finished dressing and walked over to wrap Davet in a hug.

"Are we squashing the D now?" Sid poked his head in, then stepped into the room to join the hug.

"Did they put you on youth outreach again?" Davet asked seriously.

"I'm trying to stay hip and current." Sid winked.

"You're failing on both." Fie couldn't help rolling his eyes. "More comfort, less sounding like you're a sixty-year-old trying to be current."

"Says the man old before his time." Sid reached out to rub his fingers through the grey hairs that had taken over Fie's beard. "Santa. Can I play with your sack if I'm a good boy?"

"You're on the naughty list—permanently." Davet snickered. His shoulders shook with the effort of keeping his laughter under control.

One thing they'd learnt being together was that Davet had a wicked sense of humour. He struggled, at times, to understand context. But Fie and Sid both greatly enjoyed the snarky comments he shared with them.

It's the purest sign of his trust and love that he's willing to be playful and not hide behind a mask with us.

The past year had brought a few changes to their lives. Good and bad ones. Sid's father had passed away. The two had reconciled before the end, leaving Sid devastated and also with a stark reminder of how short life could be.

They'd made a massively life-altering decision—moving in together.

Sid and Davet had moved into Fie's cottage, mostly because he didn't fancy living in either a tin can or Sid's apartment-cum-hovel. They'd expanded his place a bit, adding a sunroom on the back for Fox and Rabbit. It also provided a quiet space for Davet, who'd disappear to listen to music and read when overwhelmed.

And somehow they hadn't lost their minds after six months together in the same home.

With a rabbit.

And a fox.

And a dog who loves country music.

The other massive change had been to Coffee First. Davet had returned his cottage to his uncle and auntie. They'd built a tiny house in the field next to Fie's workshop, added multiple tables with umbrellas, and restarted the coffee shop a stone's throw from home.

At first, Fie had worried about the effect on his stress levels between the coffee shop customers and sharing the cottage. He'd been surprised when everyone respected the privacy of his workspace. Davet and Sid in bed with him every night had more than made up for any added anxiety.

"Earth to Fie. Can you hear us?" Sid snapped his fingers in front of his face. "You all right? You've been spaced out all day."

Fie glanced between the two men still pressed up close to him. He squeezed them closer, leaning forward so their heads rested together. "I love you."

"Oh, good. I was worried we'd gone and moved in for no reason whatsoever." Sid wiggled slightly when Davet poked him in the side. "That's assaulting an officer."

"With a finger."

Fie grinned at Sid while Davet seemed oblivious to their amusement. "I will pay you a hundred quid to file a report indicating you were assaulted by finger."

"How many fingers?"

"Are we talking about sex again? With visitors outside waiting on us?" Davet tended to prefer not to be overtly sexual around others; public displays of affection made him intensely uncomfortable. Fie and Sid both did their best not to make social occasions any harder on him.

"We'll leave the finger inspection until later." Fie drew Sid into a searing kiss, then Davet. He made sure they indulged his voyeuristic urge to watch them as well. "Ready to face the troops?"

An hour later, Fie leaned against the fence, watching his friends playing a rowdy game of crocket, a game Sid had invented combining cricket and croquet that only made sense in his mind. They all seemed to be enjoying themselves. He didn't know if anyone had actually figured out the rules.

On the opposite side of the garden, Davet had made a quiet zone for himself. He had Haggard, Fox, and Rabbit with him along with the latest novel for his book club for two. Fie and Sid usually went out for dinner when Shirley came over for their weekly meeting.

"Swayze."

Fie saluted Jane with his glass when she extracted herself from the chaos to join him. "Not interested in the game?"

"Are you happy?"

He blinked in surprise at the question. "Pardon?"

"Happy?" She hopped up to sit on the fence, elbowing him in the side. "Are you happy with your two men?"

"Blissfully."

Despite Jane's attempts to prod more information

out of him, Fie continually changed the subject. Eventually, he wandered over to collapse on the grass next to Davet, resting his head on his leg. Sid joined them not long after, finding a space on Davet's other side.

"Who won?"

"No idea. I forgot the rules." Sid rolled slightly to rest his head on Davet's thigh. His head bumped against Fie's. "Can we send them home?"

"No." Fie closed his eyes to block out the bright afternoon sun. "Jane asked if I was happy."

"Are you?" Sid asked. He occasionally had bouts of insecurity that always surprised Fie. He'd expected himself or Davet to suffer most with doubts. "With us?"

"As happy as the day you literally shouted in the middle of supper with your father how much you were in love with Davet and me," Fie teased.

He'd never forget that night. They'd been in the middle of the most awkward meal when Sid burst out in the restaurant with his declaration. The bigger surprise came from Davet, who'd quietly admitted to having fallen deeply in love as well.

Fie had taken longer. He'd been afraid of saying the words after his failed previous relationship. Now, he revelled in the love that swirled around them. "I've never been happier. I can't imagine a time when I would be."

Blissfully happy in love.

What better way to spend the rest of our lives together?

THE END

THANK YOU

Thanks for reading *At War with a Broken Heart*. I hope you enjoyed the story. I appreciate your help in spreading the word, including telling a friend. Before you go, it would mean so much to me if you would take a few minutes to write a review and share how you feel about my story so others may find my work. Reviews really do help readers find books. Please leave a review on your favorite book site.

Don't miss out on New Releases, Exclusive Giveaways and much more!

JOIN MY NEWSLETTER:
eepurl.com/Q0n0X
LIKE ME ON FACEBOOK:
www.facebook.com/dahliadonovan
JOIN MY READER GROUP:
www.facebook.com/groups/1326515147425106
FOLLOW ME ON TWITTER:
www.twitter.com/DahliaDonovan
FOLLOW ME ON PINTEREST:
www.pinterest.com/dahliadonovan
FOLLOW ME ON GOODREADS:
www.goodreads.com/author/show/8184061.Dahlia_Donovan

Follow me on Instagram:
www.instagram.com/dahliadonovanauthor
Visit my website for my current booklist:
www.dahliadonovan.com

I'd love to hear from you directly, too. Please feel free to email me at dahlia@dahliadonovan.com or check out my website www.dahliadonovan.com for updates.

Other Books by Dahlia Donovan

If you loved *At War with a Broken Heart*, you might enjoy the other witty, real, and romantic stories and books Dahlia has published.

List Of Books

THE GRASMERE TRILOGY:
Dead In The Garden
Dead In The Pond
Dead In The Shop

THE SIN BIN SERIES:
The Wanderer
The Caretaker
The Botanist
The Royal Marine
The Unexpected Santa
The Lion Tamer
Haka Ever After

STANDALONES:
After The Scrum
Forged In Flood
Found You
One Last Heist
The Misguided Confession
All Lathered Up
At War With A Broken Heart

ACKNOWLEDGEMENTS:

A massive thank-you to my brilliant betas who take my first draft and help me turn it into something legible. To Becky, Olivia, and all the fantastic people at Hot Tree. And also to my beloved hubby who keeps me from losing my mind while I'm stressing over word counts.

And, lastly, thank you, readers, for following me on my writing journey. I hope you enjoyed *At War with a Broken Heart*, even if you needed a box of tissues to get you through the storms to the blue skies on the other side.

ABOUT THE PUBLISHER

Hot Tree Publishing opened its doors in 2015 with an aspiration to bring quality fiction to the world of readers. With the initial focus on romance and a wide spread of romance subgenres, Hot Tree Publishing have since opened their first imprint, Tangled Tree Publishing, specializing in crime, mystery, suspense, and thriller.

Firmly seated in the industry as a leading editing provider to independent authors and small publishing houses, Hot Tree Publishing is the sister company to Hot Tree Editing, founded in 2012. Having established in-house editing and promotions, plus having a well-respected market presence, Hot Tree Publishing endeavours to be a leader in bringing quality stories to the world of readers.

Interested in discovering more amazing reads brought to you by Hot Tree Publishing? Head over to the website for information:

WWW.HOTTREEPUBLISHING.COM